A
Little
Demonstration
of
Affection

———

A
Little
Demonstration
of
Affection

_____

by Elizabeth Winthrop

Harper & Row, Publishers

New York · Evanston · San Francisco · London

For
Mummy and Daddy

———————

Chapter One

John started planning the hole that spring. In Jenny's mind, it was always *that* spring before *that* summer. The summer when the people in her life changed places and she looked at them in different ways. It was only when she thought about it later that Jenny realized how many things exploded inside her the summer of the hole.

John called a meeting in the cellar so that he could explain his idea to her and Charley.

"I'm going to dig it on the other side of the driveway wall above the stream. I've walked all over that hill. The soil is made of very thick clay. It will hold together no matter how deep we go."

Jenny picked up a hammer and started tapping it lightly against the table. It had been a long time since they had all met in the cellar. "But why do you want to do it?" she asked.

"It will be our secret place. We can go down there without Ma and Pa bugging us." He looked at Charley. "What do you think? If you guys don't want to help, I can get Andrew and some of the other kids from school. I just thought I'd let you in on it first so you can use it too."

"You mean so we can dig it," Jenny muttered. She was surprised. John hadn't gotten involved in a project since building the treehouse last summer. He barely talked to her anymore. And he had never paid much attention to Charley.

"It's a great idea, John," Charley said eagerly. "But how are we going to get the dirt out of the hole?"

John leaned across his desk and pulled out a pad of paper. He drew a picture of the hole. "I plan to put it right beside this tree here next to the wall. That's the deepest part of the hill. Then we'll hook up a pulley system with buckets between two trees. You fill a bucket with dirt and run it down the hill on a rope. At the bottom it knocks against a tree and the dirt dumps out above the stream. The weight of the full bucket going down pulls the empty one up."

"That's fantastic," Charley said.

"I've been planning this for a while," John said.

Jenny sighed. Charley always thought everything John could do was amazing, and John loved to hear him say it. "Are you going to ask Ma and Pa about it?" she said.

John and Charley exchanged glances. "There you go again," John said. "Always worried about what they're going to think. Who cares? It's not in the house. That's why I'm doing it. To build something outside they can't lay claim to. It'll be our place."

"It's on their property. And you'll be using their buckets and their ropes, and you're dumping the dirt in their stream."

"Oh, forget it," John said, throwing his pencil down on the desk. He needed Jenny to help. Charley always got asthma in the spring, and he never stuck to something the way Jenny did.

"Look, Jenny, do you want to help or don't you?" Charley said. "If you don't, clear out and leave us alone. But if you're in, it's all the way. No complaints, no whining."

Jenny laughed. "Who are you, the foreman on this job? I haven't noticed you around the place before."

Charley blushed. They had never asked him to help before. This time he really wanted to show them he could keep up with them.

"All right, I'll help," Jenny said. "I'm pretty sure you couldn't do it without me. Anyway, I don't have anything better to do."

"Oh how wonderful," John said. "We're so honored to have your esteemed company and your priceless advice."

Jenny glared at him. His sarcasm hurt more now, because he never used to talk to her like that. They used to be partners. Equal. Until Andrew came along.

"Come on, you two, cut it out or we'll never get anything done," Charley growled. "When are we going to start, John?"

"This afternoon we'll hook up the pulley system. I've got some rope down here. You hunt around for the buckets. We need two metal ones."

"Shhh," Charley said softly. "I hear someone coming." They sat in silence. Down the stone corridor they heard footsteps.

"Ma?" Jenny called.

Moses, Charley's black Labrador, appeared around the

corner. "God, Moses, you scared us," Charley said sheepishly. John looked at Jenny and raised his eyebrows. They both thought Charley was a little nutty about his dog.

"You'd better keep him out of the way when we get to work," John warned. "I remember last year he kept trying to follow us out on the roof when we were building the treehouse."

Jenny wandered away. She loved poking around in the musty rooms of the cellar. Soon after they moved into the house, Pa had divided up the cellar among the three children. Charley had sold his part to John for an old aquarium. He never liked the cellar as much as Jenny and John did. The dank air gave him asthma. John's section had three rooms: one for chemistry, one for electronics and then the central room with the old rolltop desk where he did all his planning. Jenny and John used to spend a lot of time down there together, mixing up chemicals and testing light waves on the oscilloscope John had bought for himself one year. Two years ago they had run the private telephone wire through the storm sewer, and then last year they had planned and built the wooden treehouse outside Jenny's bedroom window. Jenny smiled to herself at the picture of them bent over the elaborate drawings of levels and ladders laid out on the old desk. In the end they had agreed to simplify it because Pa was afraid the heavy beams might damage the tree they had chosen.

She passed the door to Ma's furniture-making room. Jenny used to love to give her friends the tour. "You mean your mother makes furniture? Gee, that's neat."

Jenny opened the door to her own room and stood there looking into the dark space. The old dollhouse stood dustily on its platform. Pa had given it to her the Christmas she was eight.

"I found it in an antique store," he said eagerly as she pulled the wrapping paper away from the gabled roof. "It's Victorian," he said, getting down on his knees beside her. "It's got three stories and a tower room over here on the side. I've bought some of the furniture for you. You have to be careful with it because the pieces are fragile. They're from the same historical period as the house."

Ma had smiled at him. "Most fathers go out and buy dolls for their daughters, but my husband, the architect, buys a dollhouse."

Pa was watching Jenny's face as she peered through the windows.

"Is it all right?" he asked quietly. "Do you like it?"

Her eyes were shining. "It's just perfect," she said slowly. "It's just exactly what I want." And it was.

She turned the light on and sat down on the floor beside the house. They had furnished every room carefully, choosing each piece of furniture as if they were going to live with it. Together they had gone around to museums and old houses, studying the way people lived in that time. It became a joke with the rest of the family, and the boys learned to leave them alone when Pa came home from work with another catalogue. Jenny had never put people in the house. She imagined that she and Pa lived there. But after a while the house was full of furniture, and Jenny began to spend all her time with John.

John was always planning some new project. He poked around the house, discovering secret places and building hideouts. The time he found the dark crawl space under the hall stairway, he asked Jenny to explore it because he couldn't fit between the narrow copper pipes. After that he began to rely on her for help.

Whenever they went to Pa to okay a new plan, he would offer his help. "I could run in the flooring for you," he would say eagerly. But John always said no.

"Why don't we get him to help?" Jenny asked once when they couldn't get a piece of lumber into the right place. "After all, he is an architect."

But John was too proud. "We should do this all ourselves. It wouldn't be our treehouse if Pa built it with us. Now try lifting the wood in the middle. It'll be balanced better." And somehow the two of them would solve the problem themselves. Sometimes it made her sad because she spent so little time with Pa.

But then Andrew had started coming over, and Jenny realized that John didn't want her around.

"Tell your sister to stop hanging around here all the time," she heard Andrew say one afternoon. "After all, this is your part of the cellar, isn't it?"

She stopped in the corridor waiting to hear John say something to defend her. But he had just quietly agreed. She left them alone from then on. John stopped coming up to the treehouse, and she moved his stuff out and took it over. He didn't even notice.

She stood up and walked out, turning the light off behind her. This whole cellar is where I used to be, she thought. I don't belong here anymore. For the first time since we moved here, I don't feel right with myself anywhere in this house.

The house had meant something special to each of them. They had rumbled and rambled around inside of it, staking their claims and then abandoning their territory. The house gave each of them room to change and move, to be alone and to come together.

Jenny climbed the stairs to her room. She threw herself down on the bed. Until now, we all belonged here. But now John is restless, and I'm looking for something I'm not finding anymore. Maybe that's why John is building the hole. "Maybe we're outgrowing this house," she said out loud. But as soon as the words were out, she wanted to take them back.

They set up the pulley system after lunch. Charley and Jenny went down to the bottom of the hill by the stream, while John stood up by the driveway. She held the ladder when Charley crawled up to hook the turnbuckle around the lowest branch of the tree. With the other hand, she held Moses by the collar.

"Charley, yell at Moses," Jenny said. "He keeps trying to go up the ladder."

"Get down, Moses," Charley said sternly. The dog dropped to his feet, whining softly. "Put both hands on the ladder, Jenny. It feels shaky."

"I've got it," she said.

When Charley had his end hooked up, he yelled up to John. Then he scrambled down the ladder, and they stood back as the first bucketful of dirt came rocketing down the rope. It crashed into another tree halfway down the hill, and the dirt spilled out.

"What happened?" John yelled. "I couldn't see."

"It hit another tree. You'll have to move the rope," Charley yelled back. "Over that way." He waved to the right.

The rope went slack and changed direction slightly. It tightened up again.

"All right?" John shouted.

Charley looked up the line. "Okay. We'll send the bucket back up." He went up the ladder again and hauled on the rope until John shouted.

Jenny watched his body as he climbed up and down. He was so thin and small that he was still wearing the blue jeans Ma had bought for him two years ago. His straight blond hair was always falling in his eyes, and he had a soft white face that turned pink in the sun. He was Ma's child in every way. She and John had Pa's coloring.

People often thought Charley was the youngest because he looked about eleven instead of fourteen. But John had come first and then Charley and then Jenny. She and Charley were only thirteen months apart. It might as well be thirteen years, Jenny thought. We barely know each other.

"What are you staring at?" Charley asked, as he stepped off the ladder. She blushed and looked away.

"Are we going to have to go up a ladder every time we want to move the buckets?" she asked quickly.

"No, he's got it hooked up lower down the tree at the top of the hill. The full bucket will pull up the empty one. Watch out, here it comes." The rope jumped and scraped against the tree with the downhill rush of the bucket. It slammed into the tree and bumped back and forth as Jenny and Charley stood watching.

"What happened this time?" John yelled.

"The bucket didn't turn over," Charley shouted back.

"It sure hits that tree hard," Jenny muttered.

Charley looked up but he didn't say anything. John came crashing down the hill toward them. His long brown hair flopped up and down on his head as his legs bumped along. He was already taller than Pa. Everything about John was loose and clumsy. Everything but his brain.

"What happened?"

Charley shrugged. "It just slammed into the tree."

"The turnbuckle's in the wrong place. The bucket should hit that branch so it turns over."

Charley nodded. He looked disappointed. "I should have thought of that."

John grinned. "You're the writer, Charley. Leave the complicated stuff to me." He crawled up the ladder and shifted the rope.

"You guys are too much," Jenny groaned. "Come on, let's try it again."

John went back up the hill.

"Sometimes John makes me furious," Jenny said quietly.

"What's going on with you two?" Charley asked, looking up the hill. "You never stop sniping at each other."

"He's just so full of himself. His I-know-so-much and you-guys-are-so . . . well . . . so-unimportant. And stupid. That kind of attitude."

"Oh, that doesn't bother me," Charley said. "He does know what he's doing." He glanced at her. "Don't be so picky about him. You never used to be."

I never used to be the left-out one, Jenny thought. You were.

"The bucket's coming down," John called.

"Stand back a little so we can see how it hits the tree,"

Charley said, bumping into her as he backed away. She felt suddenly like crying. The things she wanted to say about John lay like a lump in her chest. The way Charley bumped into her without saying anything made her ache with an angry kind of longing that she couldn't understand. I'm like a prickly pear, she thought, not even sure what that was, but knowing it sounded just right.

The bucket came crashing down the hill, bouncing crazily on the rope. It tipped over and the red-brown earth slid heavily out, burying a clump of weeds.

"It worked," Charley shouted. "It worked. It all fell out, just the way it was supposed to."

"Come on up. We'd better get to work."

The dirt was heavy and filled with rocks. Before long, they ran into the roots of the tree John had attached the pulley system to.

"What are we going to do?" Charley asked, pushing his hair back off his face.

"We'll just have to dig a little farther to the left," John said. He looked worried.

"You mean start all over again?" Jenny asked.

John shook his head. "No, the tunnel down will just have to be a little crooked."

"Won't it cave in?"

"I can't tell yet. We won't know until we go down deeper."

After another couple of buckets went down the hill, John decided to go check on the pile of dirt. Charley dropped his shovel and hoisted himself up on the wall. He was wheezing.

"Do you want me to get your spray?" Jenny asked. "I saw

it up on your bureau this morning."

Charley shook his head. "It's not bad yet," he said between deep whining breaths. "I just need to rest."

Jenny turned away and looked down the hill. His asthma always scared her. She still remembered the night years ago when she woke up to the sound of it for the first time. It happened in their old house where they all slept in a big nursery room in bunk beds. She had run for Ma, and Charley had been bundled up in a blanket and carried away. He stayed in the hospital for a week that first time.

John struggled back up the hill. "The dirt's dropping in the right place. Just this side of the stream. What's wrong with you?" he asked, looking up at Charley. "We aren't even down a foot yet."

"Charley has asthma," Jenny said, kicking her foot against the lip of the shovel.

"I'll be okay in a minute."

Up above them, they heard the front door slam.

John straightened up. "It's Pa," he said quietly. "Let me do the talking."

At the bottom of the porch steps, Pa stopped and looked at the three of them for a long time without saying anything. Jenny loved the way he looked—his ruddy face and the black hair combed straight back off his face. It was just beginning to go gray above his ears.

"What's going on here?" he asked.

"We're just fooling around," John said with a shrug.

"You fool around pretty seriously," Pa said, nodding at the pulley wires. "Where are you dumping the dirt?" he asked, peering down the hill.

Jenny grinned. Pa knew just what was going on.

"This side of the stream," Charley said quickly. "The system works really well, Pa. John figured the whole thing out."

John glared at him.

"What's the hole for?" Pa asked, shoving his hands into his pockets. His gray pants were baggy and stained with ink. Ma always called them his Saturday pants.

John shrugged. "I thought we could use it as a bomb shelter. Something like that."

Boy, does that sound lame, Jenny thought. She pushed her shovel into the dirt again.

"I think the cellar might be a little safer," Pa said with a laugh.

"God, Pa, you don't even give it a chance," John grumbled.

"Oh, it's fine with me. Just as long as you don't damage any of the trees. And make sure that dirt doesn't block up the stream. If it starts piling up down there, you'd better think of a system to spread it out along both sides of the stream."

John didn't say anything. "Sure, Pa, we'll take care of it," Charley said quickly.

Pa looked down at him. "You sound a little wheezy," he said softly. "Have you got your spray with you?"

"I'm fine," Charley said angrily, pushing himself off the wall. He picked up his shovel and began to dig again.

Pa stood and watched them for a while before he went up to his car.

Chapter Two

The hole took over, Jenny realized later. They never did figure out why. There was no real reason for it. But once it was started, they had to finish it.

They spent every free afternoon and every weekend digging, but it went slowly. Charley's asthma was bothering him, so Jenny often dug for both of them while Charley rested. John went down the hill all the time to check on the dirt pile.

"This is a typical project of John's," Jenny remarked to Charley one afternoon when John had disappeared down the hill for the second time. "It may be his inspiration, but we do all the work."

Charley didn't say anything. He was stroking Moses' neck absentmindedly. The dog kept trying to jump down in the hole with him, and Charley knew it was driving John crazy, but he hated to lock Moses in the house.

13

John clambered back up the hill. "We've got to dig faster. I want to get down much farther before Pa checks on that dirt pile. He'll make us start spreading it up and down along the stream, and that takes too much time."

"Maybe if you did a little more digging and stopped 'checking' on things all the time, it would go a little faster."

"Oh shut up, Jenny, I'm working just as hard as you are."

Jenny sent down the bucket she had filled and walked up to the house.

"Hey, where are you going?" John yelled.

She didn't answer.

Jenny wheeled her bike out of the garage and pushed it up the big hill behind the house.

Lucy lived with her mother in a brick apartment building on Bartlett Avenue. Jenny had never forgotten their first conversation when Lucy arrived at the convent school.

"I live with my mother," Lucy said. "My father is dead. I'm not a Catholic, and he would turn over in his grave if he knew I was coming to school here."

"Well, then why are you?" Jenny asked.

"Because my mother got mixed up and forgot to enroll me in school," Lucy shrugged. "This is the only place that would take me so late in the year."

But she stayed at the convent, and she and Jenny began to spend all their time together. The nuns approved of the friendship. "Jenny has never found it easy to make friends," Mother Sessions remarked to Jenny's mother at one of their annual meetings. "And she is a good influence on Lucy, who has not had strong direction at home. She is an impulsive girl, and we believe Jenny will help her to curb her bad impulses."

The family took to Lucy very quickly. "That girl has a very funny sense of humor," Pa told Ma one night after dinner. "She is so much more relaxed than Jenny."

"With a mother like hers, Lucy would have to be flexible," Ma replied. "Jenny says she's terribly vague and unpredictable. Last week they found a washcloth in the icebox, and Mrs. Franklin had left the house with water boiling on the stove. Things like that happen all the time. Lucy seems to just take it in stride."

Jenny had been shocked and fascinated by Lucy's casual attitude toward Catholicism. She had been brought up to believe that being a Catholic was one of the most important things in her life. In the seventh grade, she toyed with the idea of becoming a nun.

"A nun?" Lucy cried. "Do you know what you are talking about?"

"Sure," Jenny said, a little annoyed. "After all, I've been going to this school for four years. I ought to know."

"No drinking, no smoking, no talking at retreats, prayers twenty-seven times a day, lights out at nine. Oh, Jenny, it's endless," Lucy groaned. "And no boys. No sex."

Jenny nodded. "I know." But she was tempted by the clean, rustling sound the habits made, and she loved the feeling of quiet holiness that came over her when she knelt in the chapel at school and looked up at the wooden crucifix.

"But why?" Lucy asked.

"I just feel it. It's not something you can really talk about."

So Lucy had started her campaign to save her best friend

from a life in the convent. She wrote her notes in study hall. "Please watch the way Mother Louise has to sit. Very straight with her hands folded." "Have you ever noticed how many pieces of clothing a nun has to wear? Watch when Mother Margaret kneels for the last prayer in study hall. There must be six or eight layers under the top robe." "Mary B. told me that the nuns get punished if they talk during dinner at night. Have you noticed Sister Cecilia hasn't been around this week?"

Jenny finally gave up the idea by herself, but Lucy always claimed complete responsibility for saving her friend from a life devoted to God.

Jenny wheeled her bike into the elevator and pushed the button for the sixth floor.

Lucy opened the door. "You're early," she said. "Come on in. Mother's out shopping."

"I got furious at John and left."

"Sounds about normal," Lucy remarked with a grin. "What did he do this time?"

Jenny dropped down on Lucy's bed. It was covered with books and a plate left over from breakfast. There were clothes hanging over the backs of the chairs and bursting out of the closet.

Jenny laughed. "Even the pictures in this room are crooked. What do you do in here? It looks as if the police have just come through searching for a secret agent."

Lucy looked surprised. She never noticed the mess.

"Do you want something to drink? Orange juice? I think that's all we've got until Mother comes back."

"That's fine." She pushed some of the clutter onto the other bed and stretched out. Lucy handed her a glass.

"What's wrong with you and John this time?" she asked again.

"The same old thing, whatever that is. I've never really figured out what suddenly went wrong, but I know John changed when he started hanging around with that creep, Andrew. Have you ever seen him?"

"That one time at your house for dinner. Remember, he sat like a stone beside your mother, and he wouldn't say anything to anybody. Even I was glad when we got up to clear the table."

"I think he looks strange. He has a sort of mean look in his eyes, and he sneers all the time." Jenny put her glass down on the bedside table.

"You're exaggerating. You make him sound like Scarface or something." Lucy grinned. "I see him all dressed up in a black raincoat and a black hat."

"He did something to John. After Andrew appeared on the scene, John started arguing with Ma and Pa and bugging me about things. He and Andrew go down and drink and smoke grass by the stream all the time." Jenny rolled over onto her stomach. "It drives me crazy because it's so put-on. John doesn't really have anything to rebel about. I mean, Ma and Pa bug all of us sometime, but basically they're pretty good parents. They know what John's up to, but I think they trust him to figure it out for himself."

"It's just a phase, my dear," Lucy said. "It will pass. How's the hole?"

"Only one of us can fit at a time now. John's supervising

and Charley's got asthma most of the time, so you can imagine who's doing all the work."

"Why do you bother?" Lucy curled up in a big chair in a corner of the room.

Jenny sighed. "Oh, you know me. Once I start these things, I can't stop until they're finished. But with John acting all strange, I feel like going away somewhere. I don't fit in right with everybody else anymore. And Charley's driving me crazy. For the first time he's really involved with one of our projects, and he's acting like King of the Castle."

"I feel sorry for Charley. He's always left out because of his asthma."

Jenny shook her head. "He likes it that way. He huddles for hours in his room, scribbling things in that notebook. God, I wish everything hadn't gotten all mixed up with the three of us. It gives me this angry kind of ache inside all the time."

"You need a man," Lucy said matter-of-factly.

Jenny blushed. "That's stupid."

"I mean it. You're too wrapped up in your brothers. You need to fall in love. We both do. And not like last time. That was ridiculous." They looked at each other and laughed. Over Christmas, Lucy's cousin and a friend of his had come to stay with the Franklins, and Lucy had decided that she and Jenny were in love with them. They followed the boys everywhere and moaned about them over the telephone and even wrote them notes once. It was only when they left that Jenny broke down and admitted that she thought Frank was an ugly name and he never brushed his teeth and his hair was too short. And Lucy had agreed that Frank was an ugly name even if he was her cousin and his friend David was very full of himself and she hated the way his pants were always too short. "We were in love with love," Lucy declared solemnly after their big confession. "The whole thing was your idea from the beginning," Jenny reminded her. "Well, next time it will be for real," Lucy said.

Jenny sighed. "I don't think I'll ever really fall in love," she said. "I don't know one person in this world I would want to be married to."

"Give yourself time," Lucy said. The front door slammed. "Come help me put the groceries away. Mother always gets it mixed up and then I can't find anything."

Lucy's mother was in the kitchen, pulling packages out of her shopping bag. "Hello, Jenny," she said softly. Jenny had never felt very comfortable with Mrs. Franklin. She seemed so vague and lost so much of the time. Lucy was the one who ran the house.

"Here, Mother, I'll put the groceries away. Mr. Halstead called you. He wants to change your lesson to Tuesday."

"Oh, I'll go call him." Mrs. Franklin's one love in life was her piano lessons. Jenny remembered one time when she and Lucy had come home early and found Mrs. Franklin at the piano. She was usually very shy about playing in front of people, but this time she had been so wrapped up in the music that she didn't hear them come in. Her fine blonde hair had slipped softly out of the bun at the back of her head, and there was the most carried-away smile on her face, as if someone had just told her a wonderful story. "Wouldn't it be great if your mother looked that happy all the time?" Jenny said. Lucy nodded. "She used to," she said simply.

When they had put everything away, Lucy pulled her

bicycle out of the closet and called to her mother. "I'm going out with Jenny, Mother. I'm having dinner at her house."

"Okay, dear. Don't get back too late. I hate your riding your bicycle after dark." Mrs. Franklin appeared at the door. "Good-bye, Jenny. I hope you'll have dinner with us soon."

"Oh yes, Mrs. Franklin. I'd like that," Jenny said quickly.

In the elevator, Lucy said with a smile, "She'll probably play the piano all afternoon. Remember when I used to feel guilty about coming over to your house so much? She really does like to be alone. She doesn't even play when it's just me around."

Jenny nodded without saying anything. It seemed to her that Mrs. Franklin was the one tragic person she had met in her life.

Charley pulled himself up on the wall. He took another drag on his atomizer and pulled the spray deep down into his chest. The taste of the spray always made him gag, but it relieved the wheezing for a while.

"Have you got it again?" John asked, looking up from his place in the hole.

"It's the season," Charley said. "You know I always get it worse in the spring."

John dug out a rock with the shovel. "Boy, great workers. One deserter and one asthmatic. We'll be lucky if this hole gets dug by Christmastime."

Moses came up from behind and pushed his face under Charley's arm. Charley scratched the dog's neck until Moses settled down beside him on the wall. Charley looked down the hill. Spring was turning into summer already, and the trees that just two weeks ago had been feathered with green were now deep with leaves. The daffodils that Ma had planted last year had bloomed and were finished. The stream was barely visible from where Charley sat. Moses stood up suddenly and jumped off the wall. He loped off down the hill, nose to the ground. Charley took another deep breath, testing the wheezes. Funny how my asthma and my dog are connected, he thought. One brought the other. Pa had given him Moses after one of his longer stays in the hospital.

"I have a surprise for you, Charley," he had told him in the car on the way home. "It's in your room."

When Charley had opened the door, there was the black Labrador puppy, snuffling and flopping over his feet. He knelt down and picked him up. The dog's feet had slipped out between his arms, and he squirmed so much that Charley barely got him over to the bed. Pa stood in the door watching the two of them.

"Well, I think you two are going to get along just fine," Pa said.

It was because he felt guilty, Charley figured out later. Pa had always felt guilty about the asthma. It had come from his side of the family, but it had skipped Pa. And now all Pa remembered when he thought of Charley was the asthma. I'm just two shriveled up lungs, Charley thought. I can't keep up with the others and Pa knows it and he feels guilty about it. He sighed. If only he would just forget it.

John had stopped digging. He looked tired.

"Hey, Charley?"

"I'm better now, John. I'll dig."

"No, that's all right. I wanted to ask you something. Andrew asked me to come and stay with him at the place his parents have up in the mountains. Somewhere in the Adirondacks."

"When?" Charley asked.

"This summer. In a couple of weeks. He said I could stay up there until school starts."

"Are you going?"

"That depends. If I went, do you think you could keep working on the hole? I mean, you wouldn't have to do it every single day, but if you got Jenny to help you, you could probably get down about ten feet. Then we could start digging out the room when I get back. You see if nothing gets done this summer, then I won't be able to finish before winter."

Charley gazed at him. Boy, I can just hear Jenny, he thought. John's going to have all the fun, and we're going to do all the work.

"Then it will be ours as much as yours, John. Jenny and I will have done most of the work."

John shrugged. "Sure, Charley. I'll let you come down anytime you want."

"You mean we'll come down anytime we want. You won't *let* us."

"Oh, come on, it was my idea."

"And it'll be our work."

"All right," John said with a wry smile. "We'll see how far you get."

You'll see, Charley thought. Maybe this is the summer I'll show them all that I'm not just the sensitive, weak brother with asthma.

22

John pulled himself up on the wall. "I'm glad I'm getting away from here," he said, looking down the hill.

"I like it during the summer," Charley said. "There's so much more room to move around in. By the end of the winter, I begin to feel trapped in the house."

"Come on, you don't even know where you are when you start scribbling in that notebook," John said. His voice was friendly.

"I'll miss you," Charley said simply. Something had changed between the two of them. Lately, John had been seeking Charley out. With three children, one was always left out, and for so long it had been Charley. Now things had shifted, and Jenny was out of place. Charley had watched her fight against it, and he felt sorry for her. But he liked being the one John turned to.

"You'll find lots to do," John said. It disconcerted him when Charley just said the way he felt. We are such different people, he thought.

"Have you asked Ma and Pa if you can go?"

John shrugged. "Oh, I'm sure they'll let me. I'll just go anyway if they don't."

"They aren't too wild about Andrew," Charley said, leaning over to scratch his leg.

John didn't say anything.

"They know about the grass," Charley said. "I heard them talking about it in Pa's office."

"You're kidding," John said, looking at Charley. "They've never said anything to me."

"That's the way they are. I guess they've decided to let you figure it out for yourself."

"Bullshit. I bet they're going to hit me with it any day

now." He groaned. "Oh God, I bet they say I can't go."

"Thought you were going to go anyway," Charley said with a grin.

"Oh, I will," John said. "I've saved up some money. I can pay for it." He was silent for a minute. "Boy, that's a drag. I wonder how they found out."

"I bet it was the time you smoked up on the roof. I could smell it in my room, and the window was closed."

"I told Andrew that was stupid, but he went ahead and did it anyway. He says his parents know, too, but they don't give a damn."

Charley smiled. John was so naive about himself. Charley was sure he really didn't want to smoke the grass or drink down in the woods or even gripe at Ma and Pa. But he never would admit what a hold Andrew had over him. "He's different from those other kids at school," John told Charley once. "He thinks for himself. He doesn't just go along with what everybody else says. He's read so much on his own that he knows more than some of the teachers. Last week he made Mr. Chapman look like a complete fool."

Charley pushed himself off the wall and started digging again. After a while John went up to the house, and Charley worked by himself until Ma called him for dinner.

Chapter Three

But as it turned out, they were all going away.

"A farm?" John said. "What kind of a farm?"

"A place up in Connecticut that your father's rented for two weeks." Ma leaned over and mopped up some water John had spilled on the table.

"We thought it would be a good idea for everyone to get out of the city for a while."

John groaned. "Oh God, another family outing."

"Is it a working farm?" Charley asked. "Horses and cows and all that?"

"I think the man next door keeps some cows and chickens. Nothing we have to worry about." Pa laughed. "I can't really see any of us milking a cow. Especially me."

"I thought you used to live on a farm when you were a kid," Lucy said. "I remember your stories about the chores."

Pa smiled. "That was only in the summers when I went to

visit my grandmother in New Hampshire. And someone was always watching me. I suppose I could milk a cow if my life depended on it," he added.

"Well, I'm sure I couldn't," Lucy said, leaning back in her chair. "They look placid, but I don't trust them."

"When are we going?" Jenny asked.

"June 15," Ma said. "Just for two weeks."

"I'll only be up there about a week," John said. "I'm going away for the rest of the summer."

"Well, this is a surprise, John," Pa said.

"Andrew invited me to go up to the Adirondacks with him. His parents have a place up there."

"You didn't tell us about this before."

Jenny saw her parents glance at each other. Charley used to call it exchanging eyeballs.

"He had to check it out with his parents first."

"I can bring Moses, can't I, Pa?" Charley asked.

Jenny frowned. Trust Charley. All he thinks about is that dog.

"Sure, Charley. We'll be driving up. You'll have to keep an eye on him. He's going to have a lot more room to run."

"Maybe I'll only stay there a couple of days," John muttered. "I don't think I can stand it much longer than that."

("You see what I mean," Jenny told Lucy later. "He irritates them intentionally. He didn't need to say that.")

"John, do you think you could ask our permission before you just take off for the summer? I was hoping you would get a job in August." Pa pushed his chair away from the table.

"Come on, Pa. I'm sixteen years old. I don't have to ask

you before I stick my foot out the door. When are you guys going to leave me alone?"

"John, going away for the whole summer is a little more than sticking your foot out the door," Ma said quietly. Jenny always thought her controlled voice was the scariest. "And sixteen years is certainly old enough to get a summer job."

John was pushing his glass around with his thumb. It hit a crack in the table and more water splashed over the side.

"Leave your glass alone please," Ma said. "This is the third time I've had to mop up the water."

"Well, why don't you just leave it there?"

"Because the water leaves a mark on the table," Ma said.

"And after all, John," Charley piped up, "Ma made the table."

That made them all smile despite the tension. Jenny stood up.

"Can we clear the table now, Ma?"

"Fine, Jenny. John, I think your father and I would like to talk to you in his office."

"I wouldn't like to be John right now," Lucy said to Jenny in a low voice.

"Nobody's ever taken into the office. Except when they're in trouble." Jenny ran some water over her plate. "The whole thing's so ridiculous. He just brings it on himself. If he had just brought up the subject differently, they would have been glad to let him go. He acts as if the whole world owes him something."

Charley put a plate down on the counter. He had a vague look on his face.

"Hey, Charley, don't you have two hands?"

"What?"

Jenny groaned. "Surely you can bring in more than one plate at a time."

"Oh, yeah, sorry," he said, before he wandered back into the dining room.

Lucy laughed. "Charley might as well be in Hawaii right now. He just tunes out."

"Sometimes I wish I could," Jenny said with a sigh.

The next two weeks for Jenny were a rushed collision of school ending and summer beginning. In the middle of final exams and the Corpus Christi procession that she loved so much and digging away at the hole, she felt the hardening of the ache inside her. Until this year, Jenny had always known how she felt about the people in her family and the house she lived in and the things that happened to her. "Now I'm not sure of anything," she wailed to Lucy, who was sympathetic but distracted. "I can't wait for John to go away, but I know I'm going to miss him. Charley drives me crazy. But just the other day he smiled at something I said, and those big goopy eyes of his smiled too, and I suddenly wanted to cry."

In the evenings after dinner, Jenny crawled out onto her treehouse. As the trees around her slowly filled out with leaves, she felt more and more cut off from the world. It's my own private bubble, she thought, I can hear only myself in here. But that wasn't exactly true. She could still hear her parents talking in low voices down on the porch. Little pieces of their conversation drifted in and out of her bubble. Little pieces of the world of the family. "We have to trust him. I'm sure he's going to hear himself one of these days, and he'll know it's not his own voice." "I sent in the deposit on the house today. They'll expect us the night of the fifteenth." "I've almost finished the table for the front porch. We'll be able to have dinner out here soon."

Jenny began to write down a list of the things that were bothering her. When she told Lucy about it, Lucy laughed. "You're the only one I know who's ever tried to organize her emotions." That was what she was trying to do. But it didn't help. Just because you write something down doesn't mean it will go away.

To Jenny's surprise, it was Charley who pinned it down for her. They were working on the hole one afternoon. John was still at school.

Jenny was sending the buckets down and Charley was digging. Moses sat on the edge of the hole whining and cocking his head. Suddenly Charley put the shovel down and stood stock still, staring at something.

"What's wrong, Charley?"

"Just a minute," he said, waving his hand at her.

She sent the last full bucket down and leaned against the tree.

Then after awhile he slowly pushed the shovel back into the dirt.

"What was that all about?" she asked.

He shrugged. "I just figured something out."

"Don't leave me in suspense," she begged.

He squinted up at her. "You won't laugh at me?"

"No," she said, looking away. His face looked so strange all wrinkled up like that.

"I think it's sad that Ma and Pa never touch each other in front of us. We've never even seen them kiss or hold hands."

She sat down on the ground in front of him and hugged her knees close to her. That was it, she realized. Or at least part of it. She suddenly remembered one time years ago when Pa had come back from a long trip out West. The children had all made a banner for him that they hung out the second-floor windows. Ma had been fluttering around the house all morning, and when they heard the taxi come into the driveway, she had turned on the children suddenly and ordered them all upstairs. "You can come down when I call," she whispered fiercely. They started out the living room door, but when Ma was outside, John pulled them all back to the window. They gathered around it giggling, just in time to see Ma throw herself into Pa's arms. He picked her up and whirled her around. That hug seemed to last forever, and inside Jenny some kind of explosion went off. She stood there staring, until John finally pulled her away and they ran upstairs just before the door opened.

"What are you thinking?" Charley asked, struck by the dazed look on Jenny's face.

"Remember that one time," she asked, "when Pa came back from that long trip?"

Charley smiled. "And we watched them out the window. That was the only time, and Ma didn't want us to see it."

Jenny trembled and she hugged her knees tighter. "It's strange, isn't it? They never touch us either."

"Remember when we used to take baths together?" Charley grinned.

Jenny blushed. "Come on," she growled. "Let's get back

to work. John will be here any minute."

But she didn't forget what he said. During the summer she thought about it often. Maybe it is the touching and the hugging that I'm missing. We're all so distant and shy with each other. But when she tried to imagine reaching out to hug Ma or Pa, the picture of it made her blush. You can't just start doing something like that, she decided. Even if you want to.

One afternoon when Jenny and Lucy came down the hill from the gym, Lucy nudged her. "Look, your father is here."

Jenny was surprised. Pa rarely picked her up at school. This was the first time all year.

She waved good-bye to Lucy and got into the car.

"Hi, Pa," she said, her voice registering the surprise.

"Your mother just didn't want to leave that table, and I was working at home this afternoon, so she asked me to come get you," he said, starting the car up.

Jenny was nervous. They had avoided being alone together lately. She was sure that Pa didn't know what to talk to her about, and she often felt the same way. Funny how the distances between two people change and grow without either of them doing anything. Except that people will always change and grow too.

"You children are really plugging away at that hole," Pa said. "You must be down three or four feet by now."

"It doesn't seem like much after all the work we've put into it," Jenny said. "I think John may have been a little ambitious this time. The earth is so heavy. I can barely lift the shovel when it's really full."

Pa smiled. "I remember Ma tried to plant a garden there

one year and nothing came up. The soil is a very heavy kind of clay."

Jenny sighed. "I wonder why we're going to all this trouble. I mean, there's no real purpose to it."

"What does John say the hole is for?

Jenny paused. She decided to tell him the truth. "He says he wants a place to get away from you guys."

"I guess the house isn't big enough for all of us anymore," Pa said with a smile.

"It's so ridiculous," Jenny muttered.

"I've gotten used to you and John by now. You just have to improve on things. The treehouse and the cellar and the private phone line. Maybe I've given birth to the architects of the future."

Jenny didn't say anything. Pa was determined to be light about John with her. The unspoken family rule of silence. She watched a bicyclist weaving in and out among the cars. Pa switched lanes and moved up toward the light. They were still a long way from home. Jenny opened one of her books and stared at the page without reading it.

"With two such energetic children, I don't know what we would have done without that house," Pa said. He pushed the hair back off his forehead with his right hand. It was a familiar gesture. "It does give us a lot of room to breathe." He looked over at her. "Elbow room."

She smiled at him suddenly. It occurred to her that maybe Pa had wanted to pick her up at school.

"What's your favorite place in the house?" she asked.

"My office. I like having the windows all the way around. That way, I can see the squirrels robbing the bird feeder and watch the garbage men leave half the garbage behind and scream at Moses when he walks right over the one tiny patch of grass I planted the week before." He laughed. "All around me I can see the disintegration of my estate."

Jenny smiled at the thought of him sitting up there. "I've never even been in the office," she said. "Except for lectures."

"I know. It's gotten a very bad reputation. But I remember when we first moved and I was working at home all the time, everybody used to troop through and I never got any work done. So I had to put it off limits."

He turned into the driveway. Jenny rolled down the window and grabbed at a rhododendron leaf as they swept past. She missed. That was bad luck.

As the car rolled to a stop, Pa turned to her. "For you, my dear, because of valuable services rendered both in and out of the line of duty, I extend to you the privileges of my office. You are welcome to come in and enjoy the view any time."

Jenny nodded. Pa hadn't used that silly tone of voice with her for a long time. It embarrassed her. She got out of the car and ran up to the house. Without even saying thank you, she scolded herself later. So he didn't know how happy it made her.

Chapter Four

"There's a big barn in back of the garage," Jenny said, coming up behind Charley, who was standing on the wooden porch. They sat down side by side on the steps. "It's not half as bad as the place Pa picked out last time."

Charley laughed. "There was a rustic air about that house."

"Musty is more like it. You had asthma the whole time." They looked out over the lawn which sloped down to a raggedy orchard. Off to the right-hand side, a large beech tree shadowed a corner of the lawn. Its gray trunk was covered with carved initials, their curves weathered to deep black. Down in the far left corner, they could make out the edges of an old garden. Beyond that, there was a line of pine trees and then the river. They couldn't see it from the porch, but Pa had already been down to look at it.

"It's perfect for swimming," he told them. "Not too wide with a good current."

Moses loped up to them and sat down beside Charley.

"You're going to have to stick around the house," Charley warned him. "If you go off too far you might not be able to find your way back." Moses reached up and licked Charley's chin. "Are you listening?" Charley asked sternly. The dog crouched down, his tail wagging. Charley pushed him over gently and scratched his stomach. "I mean it," he said softly.

"I don't think he's listening," Jenny pointed out. Moses' eyes were closed. He looked as if he were smiling with contentment.

"I would like to be transported back to this place a hundred years ago. Imagine our family living here then."

Jenny groaned. "I know who would be doing all the work. Me and Ma."

Charley grinned. "I can just see you in a long apron, lugging the tin pail of milk across the yard. 'Hey Maw, here's your milk. Reckon I'll git over to the chicken house now and see if them lazy chickens has laid any eggs.' "

"This is Connecticut, not South Carolina."

They were silent for a minute. Across the fields came the distant drone of a tractor. Moses snapped at a fly.

"You would be down pruning the apple trees in your britches," Jenny said.

"And John would be haying the field."

"I doubt it," Jenny said wryly. "John would probably be sitting on the fence supervising."

The screen door slammed.

"What a dump," John said. He sat down beside them.

"It's not as bad as the other one," Jenny said. "In fact, I sort of like it. After all, we can stand it for two weeks."

"Two weeks for you deprived souls. I'm leaving Saturday."

"I can't believe Pa said you could go," Charley said.

"Sure he did. He usually sees things my way."

Jenny burst into a fake coughing fit.

"What's wrong with her?" John said.

"I don't know," Charley said with a shrug. "Maybe she's allergic to New England."

"Maybe I'm allergic to my brothers," Jenny gasped. "One in particular who sees fit to lecture constantly to his deprived siblings."

"Who could she be talking about?" John asked earnestly.

"Beats me," Charley said with a shrug. "Must be someone she knew in her former life."

"I think I'll go unpack," Jenny said, standing up. But she wasn't really mad. Maybe a new place changes the way people react to each other, she thought as she lugged her suitcase up the stairs.

The room she had picked out looked down toward the river. From her window, she could almost reach the longest branch of the beech tree. What a great treehouse tree, she thought, gazing down into the crisscross of branches. She smiled at herself. Maybe Pa is right. Maybe I will be an architect.

She pulled the clothes out of her suitcase and laid them neatly in the bureau drawer. Pa stuck his head in the door.

"So this is where you are. How's the view?"

Jenny waved at the window. "I can almost see the river."

"I think this green ivy wallpaper crawling around would

drive me crazy after a while," he said, opening the closet door and peering inside.

"It makes me feel protected," Jenny said. "Like the bottom bunk in a bunk bed. Over here someone wrote his name on one of the leaves. David."

Pa started out the door. "I'm doing a tour. You want to come?"

"Okay. I've finished unpacking."

They prowled through the house, opening doors and peering into cupboards. It was a big house, but the bedrooms were small and low-ceilinged. "Built about 1820, I think," Pa said. "The rooms were small because they held the heat better."

"You could do a lot with this house if you really fixed it up," Jenny said, running her hand over a worn spot on the living room sofa. "The furniture is so ugly." The dollhouse suddenly popped into her mind, but she didn't mention it.

"Look at this," Pa said. He was pointing to a square open space beside the living room fireplace. "I bet they used to bake bread in here. See, there's another one down below."

"I wonder if there's a secret passage somewhere in this house," Jenny said softly, eyeing the panels above the fireplace.

The cellar ran the length of the house, and the stone foundation walls twisted back and forth into tunnels. It smelled like chalk. They came up a flight of steps to a locked door. Ma answered their banging, and they found themselves in the kitchen.

"Quite a house," Pa said, wiping some dust off his cheek with his handkerchief. "It must have been built in the early nineteenth century."

Ma laughed. "Well, I don't think the stove's been used since then. I found a mouse nest in the broiler."

Jenny looked at both of them. Their enthusiasm made her smile. Ma's blonde hair fell in curls around her face, and she kept brushing it away impatiently. Her forehead was streaked with dirt. Pa handed her his handkerchief. Jenny suddenly turned away and went upstairs. She felt left out.

She pushed open the window and propped herself up on the sill, her feet dangling over the side. She could see John and Charley walking down toward the river, with Moses loping along behind. Charley was only a little taller than John's shoulder. He had to take almost two steps to John's long one.

Charley had told her about his conversation with John about the hole.

"Oh, dammit, Charley, he's just got us doing his work for him."

"I know what he's trying to do, but it's going to be our place as much as his. I figure with you and me doing some work on it every day, we can finish the thing by the time he comes back. Then we'll be the ones who will be letting him come in."

Jenny kept shaking her head, but she knew she would help. Charley couldn't possibly do it without her. His asthma seemed to be getting a little better, but he couldn't dig for more than twenty minutes at a time without having to rest. Besides that, there was nothing else for her to do. Lucy had gone away too. In the summer she worked as a counselor in a girls' camp. Before they had left for the farm, Jenny had gone over to say good-bye to her.

"Boy, am I going to miss you," Jenny said. "It looks like it's going to be me and Charley all summer."

"Things could be worse," Lucy said. "It could have been John." She leaned down on the top of her suitcase, but it wouldn't shut. "Now what can I leave behind?" she said, eyeing the overflowing pile of clothes.

"You'll come back all tan and blonde, and I'll look like a cauliflower from slaving away in that hole all summer."

Lucy laughed. "Well, just stay out of the hole then. You haven't signed any construction contracts, have you?"

Jenny didn't answer. She knew she would help Charley. She just wasn't sure why.

John left on Saturday. Andrew and his parents stopped by to pick him up. Ma asked them all in for lunch, but Andrew's father said they had to get on the road.

"Well, how about something to drink at least," Pa said.

"That might be a good idea, Frank," Mrs. Carlton said timidly. She was a small woman. Jenny wondered if she had to sit on a pillow to see over the steering wheel. They decided to stop "just for a minute," and John took Andrew through the house. Jenny tagged along.

"What a dump," Andrew said, stepping over the hot-air grate in the front hall.

"See what I told you?" John said. "Pa has a natural talent for picking them. This is a palace compared to the last place."

Jenny walked along behind, her fists clenched. Already she felt as if this were her house they were talking about. She hated Andrew's sliding, sloppy walk and the way his dark hair curled up in back. Most of all she hated the way John sounded when he was around him. But she kept quiet because she knew John would send her away if she said anything.

They walked along the upstairs hall, opening the doors and sticking their heads in.

"Man, give me modern living any day over something like this," Andrew said. "These creaky old monuments give me the creeps."

When they came to her room, Jenny slipped in front of the door. She didn't want their rude faces poking into her place.

"Private," she said quickly.

"Knock it off, Jenny," John said, trying to push her aside.

"What have you got hidden in there?" Andrew asked. "Some secret lover?"

Jenny blushed and tightened her grip on the doorknob.

John shrugged. "Come on, Andrew, skip it. That room just looks like all the others. I want to show you the attic."

Andrew winked at her just before he turned away. She slipped inside her room and locked the door behind her. "What a creep," she said out loud. She stayed up there until she heard the car drive away.

"Why didn't you come down to say good-bye to John?" Charley asked later.

"I was busy," she said quickly.

"Sorry I asked," Charley muttered.

After John left, there was an easiness among the family that they all noticed. "Like a great big sigh of relief,"

Charley wrote in his notebook. Ma and Pa took long drives out in the country, looking at houses and poking through antique stores.

"Pa almost bought us an organ today," Ma told the children at dinner one evening. "Actually the store owner said he would throw in a top hat for free, and I think it was the top hat he really wanted. I had a hard time restraining him."

"That would have been neat, Pa." Charley said. "Our house would have sounded like a church."

"Except none of us can play it," Jenny pointed out. "We're all tone deaf."

"Not all of us," Ma reminded her gently. "That trait comes from your father's side."

Charley took long walks with Moses through the woods. He found a big flat rock off one of the paths, and in the early afternoon he could lie there in the sun and write in his notebook, while Moses rambled off by himself. He put down descriptions, pictures of people and places. "When Jenny gets mad, her lips tighten up into a thin line. She looks as if she might swallow up her face." "In the fall, the twilights are green and the flies die, buzzing circles in the dusty corners of the house." He had been working on that sentence for a long time. Finally it seemed right. "In the evenings, the crows call back and forth to each other from the trees. The crickets buzz and scratch from their hidden places in the fields, and in the distance a dog barks. Sometimes it's even noisier here than in the city."

He had been trying to write a real story for a long time, but the plot was always forced and the characters sounded made up. It bothered him. "You can't be a writer if you just write little snatches of unconnected things," he told Moses one afternoon. The dog lay down on his belly and inched slowly toward Charley, whining softly. Charley laughed and hugged him. "You always know just what to say," he whispered into the musty fur. And they went off for a long walk.

When they came out of the woods behind the house, Charley saw Jenny sitting at the top of the long hill that looked down toward the neighboring farmhouse. He stood watching as Moses broke away and bounded up to her. Jenny turned and waved.

"Wherever Moses is, you can't be far behind," she said, as he came up.

He sat down beside her. "We've been on a long walk," he said.

"Your cheeks are all red," she said, glancing at his face. "I went swimming in the river. It's great today. The sun comes down through the trees. It keeps your face warm when you float. You have to be careful, though, because the current is really strong in some places."

He looked away. Would she have said that to John, he wondered. Do all of them just sit around and worry about weak little Charley? Moses stood up suddenly and ran down the hill, barking furiously. Charley called after him, but the dog didn't turn around.

"There's a woman down there," Jenny said. "See, she just came out of the back door. Call him again."

Charley stood up and shouted, but Moses had disappeared around the corner of the barn.

"Come on," Charley shouted, starting after him. Jenny

hesitated and then plunged after them through the long grass.

When they came up, breathless, they found the woman holding Moses by his collar and shouting at him. She looked furious.

"I've seen this dog around," she said to Charley. "We got livestock here. This here is a farm. We don't want any trouble, so you keep your dog on a leash. I don't want him chasing my animals. These city dogs don't know how to act on a farm."

Charley took Moses by the collar and turned away without a word. Jenny walked away with him.

"You keep him on a leash, you hear," the woman shouted after them. "If my husband sees him, he'll go after him."

Jenny looked back once when they had reached the top of the hill. The woman was still standing there staring at them.

Charley put Moses in at the kitchen door. "What happened?" Pa asked, when he saw them walk up.

"Moses was barking at something down at that farm," Jenny said. "We went after him and the woman was furious. She kept yelling at us to keep Moses tied up."

"I think it's a good idea, Charley," Pa said, glancing at him. "Mr. Woodruff warned me about that man. He said he's very unpredictable."

"Moses hates being locked up," Charley said quietly.

"It's for his own good," Pa said.

"God, we might as well be at home. He has more room to run there," Charley said, as he went up the steps.

Pa looked at Jenny and raised his eyebrows. She shrugged and went outside.

"Ma, you want to walk down to the river with me after we finish the dishes?" Jenny asked. "I want to show you this place I found. I think the fishing would be good down there."

"Sure. I'll bring my rod." Her mother opened the cabinet door under the sink and peered in. "I think we have a leak," she said.

Charley handed Jenny another plate to put away and ducked down beside his mother. Jenny smiled at the sight of their two bottoms resting on their four ankles. Ma and Charley always accepted each other easily. There never seemed to be any distance between them. Just being alone with Ma meant a lot to Jenny, but they often found it difficult to be natural with each other.

"Jenny, bring me the tool kit, will you?" Ma asked. Her voice echoed out from the cavern under the pipes.

Jenny got the tool kit and slid it in beside them. Her mother picked out a wrench and some pliers.

"Here, Charley, you hold that there and I'll tighten this."

Jenny smiled again. Pa may be the architect, but Ma was the one who knew how to fix things around the house.

Charley backed out just as Jenny was putting the last dish away. "Ma fixed it," he said proudly.

"And you got out of finishing the dishes," Jenny said wryly.

"I helped her," he said indignantly.

Pa came into the kitchen. "I thought we'd all go swimming. There's another hour of light left."

Jenny frowned. She had planned the fishing expedition specially.

"Jenny and I are going fishing," Ma said briskly. "Charley, will you put away the tool kit, please?"

"Guess it's you and me, Charley," Pa said slowly. "You want to go?"

"Sure," Charley said, "I'll be down in a minute." He put away the tool kit and ran up the stairs to put on his bathing suit before Pa changed his mind.

The night was hot, and in the distance they could see flashes of lightning in the thunderheads.

"It will probably pour just as we're settling down on the riverbank," Ma remarked.

"Aren't the fish supposed to be hungry in the rain?"

"I have good luck on a drizzly afternoon, but I think they head for the bottom in a thunderstorm." She smiled. "If I caught a couple we could have them for breakfast." Jenny glanced at her mother. She had pushed her hair back with a headband, but the stubborn curls slid forward toward her face. Her wide, dark eyes seemed to be smiling. Sometimes she looked so much like Charley that it startled Jenny.

"What are you looking at?" Ma asked.

Jenny blushed. "I was thinking how much you look like Charley. You both have that same goofy grin."

"I'll take that as a compliment," Ma said.

"I wonder why Pa doesn't like to go fishing."

"He's too restless. I used to fish with my father, and he taught me how to be still. Pa thinks if you're not working you should be engaging in some sort of violent exercise. Remember those endless bike rides we all used to go on?"

Jenny laughed. "Pa was always staring so hard at the buildings that he kept running into people. It was dangerous to be out on the streets with him."

They walked in silence for a while. Jenny's sandals flapped softly against the dirt road. These were the times she loved being with her mother, just the two of them going somewhere and talking.

But there were so many things that Jenny couldn't talk to her mother about. She remembered the time she came home from school complaining about cramps. "Actually I just had a stomachache," she admitted to Lucy later. "But since everybody at school was talking about cramps, I just called them cramps, too. Ma called me upstairs and handed me a book called *You and Your Body* and a box of Kotex. Ma is so funny. She couldn't just sit down and explain it to me." It was all part of what she and Charley had talked about, Jenny realized. No touching, no hugging, no crying. Don't get too close.

"All right, Jenny. Where is it along the river?"

"Follow me." She slid down the bank and walked along a tiny path by the edge of the water. "I was swimming in a different place today, and I floated down here and saw this spot. Here it is," she said, climbing onto a flat rock. "See how deep the water is by here? I bet there's some deep spring that comes up from under the rock."

"Looks like a good place." She climbed up beside Jenny and settled into a comfortable position. "There might even be some trout in here."

Jenny sat still while her mother fastened a small white-and-black fly to her leader and cast the line out on the water.

The current tugged gently at it.

"That fly must look like a huge, delicious bug to any fish," Ma said happily. The sight of her mother sitting gracefully on a rock casting out her line made Jenny happy. She had always been proud of the way her mother looked and the things she could do. Ma just believed you could do anything if you tried hard enough.

"When did you learn to make furniture?" Jenny asked.

"Grandfather taught me. He used to do it as a hobby, and then when he retired, he began to sell some of his pieces. He made reproductions. You know that desk we have in the living room was one of his."

"I know. I love the secret drawers and cubbyholes in that desk."

"So do I," Ma said. "But I was never any good at that fine work. My hands are too big, and I'm not precise or patient enough. That's why I make the simpler modern furniture." She pulled her knees up to her and inched backward on the rock. "John has my big hands, but he knows how to do detailed work with them. He's not as clumsy as I am."

"The house seems so quiet now that John is gone," Jenny said. She slipped off her sandals and put them behind her. The rough surface of the rock felt cool against her bare feet.

"I hope John has a good summer," Ma said with a sigh. "He certainly has been looking forward to getting away from all of us."

"He drives me crazy with his big know-it-all attitude," Jenny exploded. "He may not be clumsy with his hands, but he's clumsy with his mouth." She stopped, pleased with the way that sounded. If I were Charley, I'd write that down in my notebook.

Ma liked it too. "That's a good way to describe him these days. But soon I hope he'll start listening to himself a little more carefully. I'm sure he doesn't mean half of what he says. You probably won't believe this, but he does care a lot about you and Charley. The difference is that Charley doesn't mind showing someone how much he cares about them. John is like Pa. Shy with his emotions."

You're the same way too, Ma. We all are, Jenny thought. Except Charley.

"Watch out," Ma said. "I'm going to cast again." When the line had curled gently out over the water, she sat down on the rock again. "There's so much caught up inside of John, so much resentment and so much love that he can't let out," she said softly. She looked away. "Tell me what Lucy's doing. I saw you got a letter from her today."

That means she thinks she's said too much to me, Jenny thought. Ma wants to be my friend, but she keeps letting the mother get in the way. Jenny pulled her knees up to her chin and said nothing. Her mother didn't press her. They sat that way for a long time, until Ma finally reeled in her line. "It's getting dark," she said. "Let's go see what Charley and Pa are doing."

They scrambled up the bank to the higher path and walked up the river. In the dusky light, the trees in the orchard looked like gnarled people standing in rows. The lights from the house set it off from the darkening fields.

"You do notice colors and seasons so much more in the country," Ma said.

"This is my favorite time," Jenny whispered. "This half light after the sun sets."

Jenny glanced at the dark shape of her mother walking beside her. *Sometimes I feel so close to her, but we never talk about the things that really count. We're so careful with each other's feelings.*

Much later in the summer, Jenny tried to explain to Charley how she felt about Ma. "We come together, we almost meet and then we veer away again. It's just like those lines on John's oscilloscope."

"I know just what you mean," he said slowly.

They found Pa standing by the bank of the river, gathering up the towels.

"Where's Charley?" Ma asked.

"He went on up ahead," Pa said. "How was the fishing?"

"We had a nice time, but I didn't even get a nibble. They must have all been sleeping at the bottom of the river."

The three of them walked up to the house together. Jenny thought it was strange that Charley hadn't waited for Pa. When Ma asked about the swimming, Pa didn't really answer.

Charley's door was shut. When Jenny knocked, there was no answer. She turned the knob and opened the door a little. Charley was already in bed, the bedspread pulled up to his chin. He was wheezing.

"Can I come in?" she asked.

He didn't answer. She shut the door behind her and sat down on the end of the bed.

"How was the swim? You look cold," she said softly.

"Oh, shut up about how I look. Everybody is always watching me. Charley looks cold. Charley's cheeks are red. Charley is wheezing." He took a deep breath and let it out slowly.

"What happened?" she asked, startled by his explosion.

He turned away and stared at the wall. They sat in silence for a long time. Jenny was about to leave when Charley started talking.

"We were swimming. We were having a good time, splashing each other and laughing. Then all of a sudden, Pa said I should get out before I got too cold. He just can't ever forget that I have asthma. He can't stop treating me like a little sick boy. So I swam away toward the deeper part of the river. The current was stronger there, but I didn't realize it until I was too far over." He paused, to breathe. "He had to come after me and pull me back. I could have gotten out by myself," Charley said angrily. "If it had been you or John, he would have just laughed. But he got that stupid, worried look on his face and he came after me. I kept pushing him off, but he wouldn't let me do it by myself."

"But the current is strong there, Charley," Jenny said. "He would have come after me, too."

Charley turned and looked at her. His chest went up and down under the bedcovers in shallow, whining breaths. She could feel his leg next to her. Some strange feeling was tickling her inside. Making her shiver a little.

"Do you want your spray?"

"I've got it," he muttered, pulling his hand out from under the covers. The green bottle was clutched in his fist. "I'm trying to get over this without it."

After a while, Jenny stood up. Charley was still looking

at her. "Well, call me, if you want anything," she said softly. "I mean if you want to talk or anything." She didn't want him to think she was treating him like an invalid. "Good night," she said, as she pulled the door shut behind her.

She sat at the window in her room for a long time. The breeze had come up and the thunder rumbled closer. The birds chattered noisily in the trees.

You're always on a seesaw with people, she thought. Me and Ma trying to talk to each other. Me and John fighting all the time and throwing everything off balance so I'm up in the air with my arms waving and that dizzy sick feeling. You swing up and down with people all the time. Then there are those still, perfect moments when everything is balanced and you both are even with each other with your pointed toes barely touching the ground. Then somebody sighs and the seesaw tips again.

She climbed down and pulled the window down as the first drops of rain spattered against it. "Now suddenly Charley's climbed onto the seesaw with me," she whispered to herself as she got into bed.

Chapter Five

Charley heard the shots first. He sat up quickly in bed and looked around his room. The rising sun made pink shadows on the shade. He lifted it and looked out. A morning mist lay in the fields. He got up and tiptoed next door to Jenny's room. She woke up as he opened the door.

"Did you hear them?" he asked in a low voice.

"What?" she mumbled.

"I think I heard shots. Coming from across the field."

"It's probably just a truck backfiring. Go back to sleep. It's still dark outside."

"I'm going to look. I let Moses out sometime in the night and he hasn't come back."

She sat up slowly. "You're always worrying about that dog. You'll never find him out there."

"I'm going to look anyway. Will you come with me?"

He looked scared. She got out of bed and pulled her jeans

on over her nightgown. They tiptoed down the dark hall. Everybody else was still asleep.

"There. Do you hear them?" he whispered. "There they are again. I'm sure it's shots."

She didn't answer. It didn't sound like a truck after all.

"They're coming from down there." He pointed down the hill. The farmhouse looked pink in the sunrise.

The long, wet grass slapped against their pants, leaving dark marks on the cloth. She shivered. The morning air felt cold. The land had evened out. The house looked empty and still.

She touched Charley's arm.

"Where are we going? I don't want to get too near the house. That woman might hear us."

He motioned to her to be quiet. "I hear a voice," he whispered. "Listen."

The sound was coming from behind the house. It was a low, threatening voice.

"Let's go," she said. "I don't like this."

"I'm going up to look," he whispered. "You stay here. Duck down in the grass."

He had gone up ahead before she could answer. She crouched in the grass, shivering in her wet jeans. When she lifted her head to look for him, he was standing at the corner of the house. Then he disappeared. She crouched down again, moving the damp grass away from her face.

The scream was such a sudden sound in the morning air that she gasped in surprise. It came again, this time a long, trailing scream that hung in the air. He stumbled by her, floundering in the long grass.

"Charley, what was it? What did you see?" She pushed after him but he would not stop.

"Pa! Pa!" He was running and screaming. Behind her, she could hear someone coming, but she did not turn around. Up the hill, the screen door slammed. Pa stood at the front steps staring at the children stumbling up the hill toward him. As Charley threw himself at his father, she could see Pa still staring at the field behind her. Finally she stopped and turned around.

The farmer was pushing through the grass, swinging a dark lump in front of him. He came toward her without stopping, flattening the long stalks with his feet. She stared at the lump dangling from his tight fist, bouncing with his walk. It was Moses. His head hung awkwardly to one side. There was blood dripping out of his mouth. She shrank back as the man swept past her. She opened her mouth to scream but no sound came out.

"This goddamned dog's been chasing my chickens. The bastard killed five of them," the man yelled, dropping the dead body at Pa's feet. Charley turned and stared at Moses. Pa tried to turn his son's head away, but the boy's head was rigid. Jenny could see him quivering. "Well, he ain't gonna chase no more," the man growled.

"You shouldn't have killed him," Pa said slowly, staring at the man's face. "I would have paid for the chickens."

"You rich folks think you can just bust in here with your dogs and your children running around," the man bellowed, looking past Pa into the house. "Just who the hell do you think you are?"

"Kill him, Pa," Charley yelled, staring up into the man's

face. "Oh, God, Moses is dead," Charley's voice cracked into crying.

"Guess you learned your lesson, boy. My wife, she warned you yesterday. She told you to tie up that dog."

"I plan to bring this up with my lawyer, you understand," Pa said. Jenny had never seen that expression on his face before. "You're not going to get away with this."

An ugly laugh roared out of the man's insides, and the long gun jiggled on his shoulder. Behind him, Jenny finally screamed. The laugh rumbled slowly into silence.

"Clear off. Get off this land," Pa shouted, stroking Charley's head absentmindedly.

"My pleasure. Be seeing you, Mr. City Folk."

The man brushed past Jenny without looking down. Charley huddled down beside Moses. He cradled the dog in his arms. When Pa leaned down to help him, Charley pulled away.

"Leave me alone," he snarled. "Don't touch him. I don't want you to touch him," he cried. Slowly he walked around the corner of the house, huddled over the dead body in his arms. Jenny sank down into the grass. She sat there for a long time, shivering. The screen door slammed, and she heard the swish of someone in the grass near her.

"Come inside, Jenny," her mother said quietly. She leaned down and pulled the girl up. Jenny stood rigidly, her bare arm pressed against her mother's side.

"He should have done something," Jenny mumbled. "He should have hit that man."

"What good would that have done?" her mother asked. Her voice sounded cracked and dry. "Moses is dead. Your father can't bring him back. None of us can. We just all have to try and forget this." Jenny looked up into Ma's face. She had been crying.

"I won't forget it," Jenny whispered. "Charley won't either. We won't ever forget it." She pulled away from her mother and ran inside. Charley's room was empty. His bed lay rumpled and open in the sunlight.

She found him outside, sitting in the door to the chicken shed. When she sat down beside him, she could feel his body shaking. He was still crying. Jenny wanted to put her arms around him. She leaned against him.

"Did you see him close up?" Charley asked. His voice sounded choked and squeaky.

Jenny closed her eyes. "Yes," she said.

"He was still warm when I picked him up. But he couldn't feel me anymore. We'll never—" Charley stopped, thinking of so many things that would never be. He cried out sharply as if in pain.

"Oh God, Charley," Jenny said, hugging her knees.

"Pa just mumbled about lawyers. He sounded like some weak old man."

Jenny looked away down the hill. "I saw his face, Charley. It was like stone. It was cold and stretched."

"I could kill that farmer. I hate him." Charley's fists were curled into his chest, as if he were trying to push something away. Jenny knew that he wanted to stop crying but he couldn't. "Oh God, what a summer. First John and now Moses—"

"I'll be home, Charley," she whispered. "We'll be together." She put her arms around his thin shoulders and hugged him, tightly, breathlessly, trying to squeeze all the pain and sadness away. Then before he could say anything, she ran away wildly, her heart beating, the ache inside of her bursting open. Charley sat on the steps, watching her go, a stunned look on his face.

Chapter Six

They drove home early, just two days after Moses had been killed. Jenny went first to look at the hole.

"I must have thought it was digging itself," she said with a laugh. "It looks so small and pathetic. After all our work." She sat on the wall and looked down through the heavy green trees to the stream. The woods rustled in the late afternoon stillness. She was glad to be home. That place had been all right, but she would never be able to think of it now without remembering Moses. The picture of that black and dangling head came rushing up at her again, and she squeezed her eyes shut. "I will think about something else," she said out loud before her throat could fill up.

She jumped off the wall and climbed down the ladder. The shovel lay where John had dropped it that last afternoon. She filled the first bucket and propped it up on the edge of the hole. She slipped once, and some of the dirt fell back in. By the time she had sent the third bucket down the hill, she was exhausted. "I'll get Charley," she thought, climbing over the wall. "We've got to get started on this or the summer will be gone before we turn around."

Charley looked at her blankly. He was sitting cross-legged on his bed.

"What are you talking about?"

"The hole. You promised John we would work on it this summer. If we want it to be really ours, we'd better get a lot done before he comes home."

Charley shrugged.

"I tried doing it myself," she explained, leaning down to look at his aquarium. "But the bucket always slips before I can get it up the ladder. I need someone to stand at the top and load up the dirt. One of these fish is floating on its side."

"I know," he said dully. "It's the Siamese fighting fish. Some of the others attacked him. I seem to have a jinx on animals," he muttered.

"Well, can't you do something for him? They're still rushing at him."

"He's going to die anyway," Charley said.

Jenny picked up one of the nets and isolated the fish on one side of the tank the way she had seen Charley do. She sprinkled some food on the water.

Charley watched her without saying anything. Usually he was very careful about his aquarium. He never let anybody touch it.

She sat down on the bed beside him. "You know, Charley, you can't just sit here not doing anything," she said slowly, tracing the design in the bedspread with her finger.

"I know how you feel—" she saw his face tighten. "Not completely. But every time I remember that day and that field, I think I'm going to choke. Everything fills up. But you'll forget it for a little if you do something. Just sitting here makes it worse."

"I don't want to forget," he said slowly, struggling over the words. "None of you will ever understand. You used to laugh with John about me and Moses. 'That dog's always in the way, Charley. Why do you always worry about that dog? Oh, you know how Charley is about that dog.' " His voice cracked and Jenny could see him struggling not to cry. She looked out the window. He was right. They had always laughed at Charley when he talked to Moses.

"You and John always had each other. Well, I had Moses," Charley said in a low voice.

"Oh Charley," she cried. She was scared by the bitterness in his voice. Suddenly she cared very much what he thought of her. "I'm sorry," she whispered miserably as she got up off the bed. "I can't finish the hole without you," she added. She really meant something else. I don't want to go through the summer without you.

He must have understood, because when he looked up at her, he smiled a little. "Thanks," he said softly.

Somewhere inside Jenny a bubble burst, and she hugged the warm feeling to herself as she ran downstairs.

Jenny went looking for Ma, but she had gone out. Down in the front hall, she stopped outside Pa's office door and listened. There was no sound. She pushed the door open slowly. Pa's drafting table was covered with blueprints, held down by tape. The red couch looked lumpy and dented, as if someone had just been sitting in it. Jenny closed the door behind her. She loved the woody ink smell of the office. Coming in here was like discovering a whole new room in the house. She curled up in the sofa and looked around.

The room was like a tower or a guardhouse with windows on three sides. Someone had added it on after the porch had been built, so that the windows on one side looked out over the porch. From Pa's desk, you could see through the trees to the neighboring house. Jenny understood now why Pa was so protective of his domain here. It was a good thinking place.

She heard footsteps approaching, and she started up from the couch. Pa had told her she could come in, but suddenly she felt uncomfortable. When he opened the door, he looked startled to see her standing there.

"Hello, Jenny." His voice was a question, not a real welcome.

I'm invading, she thought, moving toward the door. He didn't really mean for me to come here.

"Don't leave, Jenny," he said. "I never go back on an invitation."

"That's all right, Pa. You probably want to get to work."

"No, I don't at all," he said, turning to her with a smile. "Now sit down and entertain me," he ordered. Pa always retreated into games. She curled back into the couch and sat there in silence as he looked through his mail.

"All junk," he said in disgust, dropping a pile of envelopes into the wastepaper basket. "Now tell me what's going on around here. How's Charley?"

"Moses meant a lot more to him than any of us realized," she said quietly. Maybe Pa had known.

"Moses was a good dog." They sat in silence. Pa twirled once on his stool. "Do you think Charley still feels the same?"

Jenny frowned.

"About me, I mean," he said brusquely.

"Why didn't you do anything?" she asked quietly.

"There wasn't anything I could do," he said. "Moses was already dead. Nothing I did would make him come back."

"But you could have made Charley feel as if you cared about it." She felt as if she were using Charley's mouth, saying the things she knew he would have said.

Pa banged on the window at two squirrels. They jumped off the feeder onto the porch railing and curled there, eyeing him. He banged again and they hopped away.

"The birds won't get anything at this rate," he muttered, turning back to his desk.

Jenny stood up to go. At the door she turned slowly. "It wouldn't hurt if you and Ma showed us how you feel sometimes," she said quickly and ran before he could stop her.

"My, Jenny, you are getting brave," she told herself as she pushed her bicycle up the hill to the street. She thought of telling Charley what she had said to Pa, but she was scared he might laugh at her. It probably wasn't such a big thing to anybody else.

Charley decided to write about it. I'm not going to get through it any other way, he thought. It will be my first real story. Dedicated to Moses. It took him a whole day to write, and once he had started he didn't leave his room. Ma tried to make him come down for lunch, but when she saw what he was doing, she left a sandwich on his bureau.

"Charley's writing again," she said to Pa when he came home that afternoon. "He's been locked up in his room all day."

"I can guess who's the villain of the story," Pa said wryly.

"I'd rather have him stab you with a pen than something else," Ma said. "I wish there was something we could do. Moses meant so much more to him than I realized."

"What about another dog?" Pa asked.

Ma shook her head. "Not now. It's too soon. Maybe he'll write some of the pain away. I'll be down in the workroom. If he doesn't want to come down for dinner, just leave him alone."

Charley finished the story that night. He read it aloud to himself and penciled in some changes. It was a whole story, he decided. "And parts of it are really good," he said out loud, as if he were talking to someone. He jumped up and went looking for Jenny. She was sitting out in the treehouse, reading by the light of a candle. When he called to her out the window, she jumped.

"God, I thought you were Ma," she gasped. "She told me not to use a candle out here."

He climbed through the window. He hadn't been in the treehouse since John and Jenny had first finished it and the whole family had eaten dinner up there. He stood at the edge looking down through the trees.

"You can't even see the street in the summer," Jenny said.

"It's nice up here," he said. "Like your own room in the forest." Now that he was there, he didn't know how to start. Maybe the story wasn't that good.

"Sit down," Jenny said. "There's room here to lean against the tree."

They sat in silence for a long time. Jenny picked up her book and started to read again. The flame of the candle bent with the breeze. Charley looked over at his sister. Her straight hair was pushed behind her ear, but as she moved her head, strands of it slipped forward. Already her face looked reddish brown. She never burned the way he did. He was glad she had let him sit there without asking any questions. The candle was burning down. Soon it would go out.

"I wrote a story about Moses," he said. She looked up. "There's just one part of it that I want to read to you. It won't take very long."

She moved the candle over so the light shifted to his face.

"Go ahead," she said softly.

Suddenly he was scared. He had never read anybody his writing before. Only Moses. He took a deep breath and started.

"When the boy ran back to the house, he could feel the field all around reaching out scratching him. He was screaming for his father who stepped through the door and stood waiting for him. The boy ran headlong into him, his face pressed against the man's robe. He kept shouting something, but no sound was coming out. On his shoulder he could feel his father patting him. The hand would just barely touch and then rise away again." Charley glanced over at Jenny's face. Her eyes were closed.

"When the farmer came up, carrying the dog's body, the boy could feel his father's body tighten. But the men just talked quietly, their voices rising up and down like gentle waves. Hello, sorry I had to kill your dog, oh that's quite all right, my son will get over it. . . . The boy could hear no anger in his father's voice, just shame. And when he struggled away with the dead dog's body, his father began to pat him again. Just the lightest touch. Don't blame me. It's not my fault. The boy wanted to scream at him, but they didn't speak or look at each other. As he threw the dirt over the dog's still body, he was struck by the silence of it all. The birds had sung and the screen door had slammed and the tractor had started up just as if nothing had happened. Only there was no dog standing at the corner of the field, barking at a toad in the grass."

He closed the notebook. I don't care what she thinks, he thought at first, but he knew he couldn't stand the silence much longer. Why didn't she say something?

"That's just the way it was," she said, leaning her head back against the tree. "I kept trying to scream, but I wasn't making any noise at all."

His body felt limp.

"Can I look at it a minute?"

He showed her the page, and she leaned over to read it in the fluttering candlelight. "I think I know what you're trying to say here at the end about the silence," she said slowly. "But you need to tie it together better. See, you say how the boy was struck by the silence of it all, but then you mention all these noises. You have to make it clear that he was struck by the silence of the death, of the dog dying."

Charley read the end of the paragraph again. "Well, he was struck by how silently the father had let it happen."

"Perfect. That's what I mean. Just a sentence," she said, smiling. "I love that last line," she added.

The candle went out suddenly, but he scribbled one line

down in the half-light from the window. He stood up reluctantly. There was no more reason to stay.

"Well, thanks," he said awkwardly. "I just thought I had to read it to somebody."

"Sure," she said. "I guess I'll come in too." They clambered through the window, one after the other, and he went through to his room without saying anything more.

The next morning Charley woke her up.

"Come on, lazybones, let's go. If we're going to get that hole finished by the end of the summer, we'd better get started."

"All right, just let me get dressed. Pour me a bowl of cereal," she yelled after him as he tumbled down the stairs.

That day they fell into a kind of routine that was to last the whole summer.

"I can just see my What-did-you-do-with-your-summer? composition," Jenny said with a laugh. "The title will be 'Various Ways to Dig a Hole.' "

"Or 'How I Found Health and Happiness in Honest Labor,' " Charley said as he sent another bucket down the hill. Jenny usually dug, and Charley filled the buckets and hooked them up.

"Charley and Jenny are spending a lot of time on that hole," Ma remarked to Pa one night as they sat on the porch.

"I'm glad," Pa said. "The house is peaceful for once. For a while there, I was really worried about Charley."

"That was a pretty hard thing for those kids to see," Ma said. "Especially Charley."

"Now don't you start," he said, smiling at her. "I've had my lecture from Jenny on the subject, and I know how Charley feels."

Ma didn't say anything.

Pa tipped his chair back. "I've never felt so helpless in my life. There wasn't a damn thing I could do. That man really was crazy."

Charley kept trying to put off spreading the dirt along the banks of the stream. "We've got to get the hole finished first. Then we'll worry about the other stuff."

But Jenny was worried. "All that dirt's going to kill the small trees and bushes unless we do something," she said one afternoon as she struggled back up the hill. He was down in the hole.

"Hand me the second shovel," she said.

"Where are you going?"

"To spread the dirt," she called over her shoulder as she went back down the hill.

"Oh, let her go," he said to himself as he slid another full shovel of dirt into the empty bucket.

After a while, she heard him calling to her. "Hey, Jenny, come back up."

"Why?"

"I can't dig by myself. I need someone to take the buckets."

She smiled to herself and went on working. Soon she heard him crashing down the hill toward her.

"All right, you win," he said grudgingly. After that, they spread the dirt every afternoon.

We had a special wave length that summer, Jenny realized much later. A kind of communication that all started with the hole. When we were in the middle of it, it was too smooth and subtle to understand. You wouldn't stop to think about it, because there was nothing to put your finger on. No signs, no footholds, just a slow, pleasant falling into each other's minds.

Chapter Seven

"The summer goes so damn quickly," Charley said vehemently.

"I know it," Jenny said. "The longest day of the year comes in June when the summer's barely started. After that, it's all downhill. It makes me think of that saying, every day is the beginning of the rest of your life." She plodded deliberately through a puddle. Her sneakers were already soaked from walking in the rain.

"You're like a little kid," Charley said with a laugh. Then he backed up and walked through the puddle himself.

"Charley, you'll ruin your sandals," Jenny cried.

"They're wet already," he said. "It feels good, doesn't it?" he asked with a smile.

She smiled back and they walked on a little in silence. Jenny remembered her mother once saying that your best friends were the people you could be quiet with.

They were walking down Bartlett Avenue. It was almost a ritual. Every day it rained in the summer, they walked down to the section of the city where the row houses lined the streets, leaning on each other, and the tiny shops were filled with dark corners and old men constantly rearranging their dusty merchandise. "It's all changed so much since we lived there," Ma had said to them that morning over breakfast. "We used to be able to hear the trolleys from the second-floor windows." "And the vegetable man came by every Wednesday in his truck," Jenny remembered. "In the summers, he used to give us a peapod each," Charley said. "Funny, the things you remember."

"Let's go by the old house now," Jenny said quickly, touching Charley's arm.

"I was thinking the same thing," Charley said.

Their old house was one of the row houses. It was connected to a yellow stucco house on one side, but the Lutheran church was their other neighbor, so there was room for a small brick path to the garden in back. The house was gray shingled, and the most recent tenants had painted the front door orange. On the second floor there was a bay window in the big nursery room where all three children had slept.

"Remember our bunk beds?" Jenny asked. "And the little set of brown chairs and the round table where we ate dinner sometimes?"

Charley nodded.

"I loved that room," Jenny said. "Sometimes I wish we had never moved."

"We had to because Ma was pregnant again," Charley said. She nodded. The baby had been born dead.

"That was strange," Charley said quietly. "The three of us so close together, and then that final lonely baby."

Their eyes met and they both looked away quickly.

"Let's go back into the garden," Charley said, starting across the street.

"What if the people are there?" Jenny said nervously.

"The place looks closed up. They haven't even taken the paper off the front stoop."

They went through the little gate and tiptoed by the house. At the corner of the garden, they stopped and looked around. In the center, there was a round goldfish pool with a tiny fountain. Gravel paths bordered with flowers meandered around the pool. One path led off to the corner where there was a small tool shed.

"It looks just the same," Jenny whispered.

"It looks smaller," Charley said.

"Things always look smaller when you grow up."

"I'm glad we moved," he said. "We couldn't have a hole or a treehouse here. It's all too small and dainty for me. Come on, let's go. I want to go to the pet store."

She followed him down the path and carefully locked the gate behind them.

Jenny loved the pet store. She could stand for hours at the tanks, watching the fish swim lazily by. Occasionally one would stop and gaze at her blankly.

"What's that one?" she asked Charley.

"A pearl gourami. I'm going to get a swordtail and another Siamese fighting fish."

"I wonder what they think we are," she said when he came back. "We must look enormous to them."

71

"Fish don't think," he said scornfully.

"How do you know?" she asked, holding the fish bag while he struggled back into his raincoat.

"I've read about them," he said. "They just react to different stimuli. Instincts. Hunger, pain."

"Humans. That big face peering at them must stimulate them."

"Well, it might make them swim away. Instinct warns them of danger. But you couldn't say a fish is scared. Only humans can be scared. Do you see the difference?"

"Sure, I do. I'm not a complete nitwit," she said grumpily. She hated that explaining sound to his voice.

"Sorry," he said with a shrug.

They walked on, stopping to peer into the dark windows streaked with rain. She bought a licorice stick at the candy store from the same old man who used to sell them candy on Sundays after church. She found Charley in the bookstore. He wanted to buy a book on breeding fish, but they didn't have enough money between them. She got bored waiting for him.

"Charley, if we don't get home, these fish are going to die. You can't sit there and read the whole book."

The rain had stopped. The wet streets shone in the sunlight. They walked home slowly.

"Do you have things in the back of your mind that you think about from time to time?" Jenny asked slowly. Charley frowned at her.

"I mean things like fish thinking. Questions that occur to you all the time and you can never really answer them."

"Like what?" he asked.

"Well, I always wonder about the way people see colors. Now you and I might both look at that stop sign and say it's red. But you might be seeing my brown. Get it?" She was watching his face for a reaction.

"Sort of. You mean, we might be seeing completely different colors, but we've both been trained to call that color red."

"Exactly. And nobody will ever be able to figure out exactly what color everybody sees, because it's a subjective reaction."

"Maybe they'll be able to do something with light waves."

"Stop," she said dramatically, covering her ears. "I don't want to know the answer."

"You're getting the licorice in your hair," he said, pulling her hands away from her head.

"Ugh," she said, disentangling it. "All right. Now it's your turn. Give me an unanswerable question. Or one you don't ever want answered."

They walked in silence for a while. "All right, here's one," he said. "Is there any part of this country that no human has ever set foot on?"

"Oh, sure," she said. "Up in the mountains and in Alaska."

"I like to think of it in a specific place we know. Take the woods up at that farm. There must be some part of those woods, some little inch, that was never stepped on by a human foot. Not even by an Indian."

"Just bugs and animals," she said with a smile.

"All right," he said, caught up in the game. "Your turn."

"Vegetables," she cried.

"What?"

"When you look at that lettuce leaf on the plate in front of you, don't you ever wonder when was the last time it saw the garden earth?"

"You're a nut, Jenny," he said with a smile. She liked the way he said it.

"Your turn," she said.

The silence was very long.

"Five minutes is the thinking limit," she warned him. "We're almost home."

"This sounds very serious," he said. "But I do think about it a lot."

"That's okay."

"God," he said simply.

"What aspect?"

"Is there one?" he said, stopping to look at her.

"You don't believe in God, Charley?" she asked, genuinely surprised. "All those Sundays we go to Mass and all those times in the confession box and you don't believe in any of it?" Her voice rose to a squeak, and she stopped to take a deep breath.

"Well, I started thinking seriously about it instead of going mindlessly off every Sunday. All these years, I've just imagined a great bearded person sitting up there somewhere. That's ridiculous."

"I know," she admitted. "That comes from the pictures in the catechism books."

"I think God is just some sort of security blanket that humans made up to get them through. I admit it is pretty horrifying to think about nothing. That the world just came from gaseous explosions or whatever and there's nothing controlling it all. We're just whirling through space with nothing looking after us."

"I believe there is a controlling force," Jenny said slowly. "There's too much order in the world for it just to have happened."

"What about the disorder?"

"Humans brought that on themselves. Maybe that was God's one mistake. He should have left us out of it completely. We're the disruptive influence because we think and change and disobey the laws." She blushed. She was saying things to Charley that she had never told anyone before. Not even Lucy.

"Well, you win first prize," she said.

"What for?"

"The most unanswerable question," she said with a laugh. "But not the most original one."

He didn't answer. He was looking at her with a puzzled expression on his face. As if he were suddenly beginning to realize that I have a brain and I do actually use it, Jenny said to herself later. It bothered her very much that Charley didn't believe in God and Catholicism anymore. She had discovered this summer that she and Charley thought the same way about so many things. Now the idea of a crack between them scared her. She didn't want him taking any trips that didn't include her. "Things between us certainly have changed," she admitted with a little smile. "Maybe without John we would have always been this way. Or maybe it's just the right time for us."

Jenny talked to Pa about it one afternoon when they were down cleaning out the stream after a storm.

The question came out suddenly, almost before she knew she was going to ask it.

"Do you believe in God, Pa?"

He looked at her with a smile. "What brought that on—working so close to nature?" he asked, eyeing the mud dripping off her hands.

"You don't have to answer," she said. "Charley and I were talking about it the other day."

"Yes," he said. "I do believe in a kind of a God. Some idea or force or being that has a hand on the steering wheel. But a very distant hand."

"What do you mean?"

"I don't believe in a benevolent person guiding us here below. And I don't believe in any one organized religion. I just believe in an indifferent force." He dug his shovel in the dirt again. "Hard to explain."

"That's sort of what I think," Jenny said. "Charley says he thinks God was made up by someone to cheer us all up. Sort of a security blanket."

"Has Charley talked to Ma about it?" Pa asked.

"I don't know," Jenny said. "Why?"

"Your mother has very strong feelings about her religion. If Charley wants to talk to someone who really knows how they feel instead of us wishy-washy people, he should talk to her."

"Sometimes Ma is hard to talk to," Jenny said timidly. "I mean about things like this."

Pa glanced at her without saying anything.

"You're not going to tell her what Charley said, are you?" Jenny asked. "I mean, maybe Charley didn't want me to mention it."

"No, I won't say anything. Come on now," he said sternly. "Less talk and more action."

They bent over their shovels again, but Jenny's mind wasn't on her work.

"How come you let Ma bring us all up Catholics if you didn't believe in it?"

Pa stared at her. "Suddenly, all these questions. Whatever happened to my shy, withdrawn daughter?"

Jenny didn't say anything.

"I thought it would be good for my children to have something definite to react against. Then you could make a choice. If you had never seen the inside of a church, then you wouldn't know whether you wanted to be there or not. And also, your mother cared very much about it," he added. "I guess that was the most important thing."

Jenny was still turning that answer over in her mind when Pa asked her a question.

"What's happened between you and Charley? You were barely speaking to each other before John left, and now you're hardly ever apart."

Jenny bent over her shovel. She knew her face was red. "Well, John and Lucy are gone. And Moses."

Pa nodded. "Oh, I see. Last two people on a desert island."

She knew he was kidding her, but she didn't say anything more. Charley called to her from the top of the hill.

"I'm back, Jenny. Come on up."

Jenny glanced at Pa. He burst out laughing. "Go on," he said. "The hole must be dug. I can finish down here."

"Thanks, Pa," she called over her shoulder as she scrambled up the hill.

The unanswerable question game went on all summer.

"Radios," Charley said to her one day when they were sitting on the wall. He was wheezing again. The humid heat seemed to make his asthma worse.

"Radios?"

"I always wonder when I hear one of those fast-talking disc jockeys whether it isn't just a tape. There's really just an old gnarled man sitting in a little dark room filled with dust and cobwebs, and all he does is change the tapes. So about every two weeks you hear the same show, but nobody ever notices."

"What a weird idea," she said admiringly.

"The only thing that bothers me is the news," he said.

"You could probably run that again in two weeks and nobody would notice," she said.

He didn't answer.

"Hey, that was a joke," she said, poking him in the ribs. "You're supposed to laugh."

He looked at her blankly. "It was pretty terrible," he said dourly.

"All right, sourpuss, back to the ditches," she said, pushing herself off the wall. She could tell his mind had suddenly switched to something else. Charley's moods were hard to follow, but she was getting used to them.

"I just saw this picture of Moses, running up the hill with his nose to the ground. You know the way he always looked when he thought he was on the trail of something," Charley said. His eyes looked glazed.

She took his hand suddenly and held it tight. Their palms were damp and covered with dirt, but he didn't pull away.

"I'm working on that story again," he said softly, looking down at her. "I'd like to read it to you."

The way he was staring at her made her tremble all over. She felt as if they were at the edge of a cliff, falling toward each other.

He pulled his hand away and jumped down quickly. "I'll dig now," he said gruffly, picking up his shovel.

That Sunday Ma sent the two of them off to church alone. She had gone to the early Mass.

"Come on, Charley," Jenny called back to him. "Father Landon always glares at the people who come in late."

Charley wanted to skip Mass. He had done it before when he went by himself, but this time he wanted Jenny to come with him. He caught up with her.

"Let's not go," he said quietly.

She looked at him.

"Let's go to the zoo instead." He had this funny secret smile on his face. Jenny knew he was challenging her. The way he was watching her made her shiver a little.

"All right," she said, pushing her hands into her pockets. "Let's go to the zoo."

They caught the bus on the avenue and rode almost the whole way without saying anything. Charley was pretending to look out the window, but he was watching Jenny out of the corner of his eye. She really is wrestling with the devil, he thought. She's trying to figure out why she suddenly cares more about what I want to do than about God and Ma and all those nuns. He pressed his nose against the dirty glass. It gave him a strange, exultant feeling to know that she wanted to follow him.

"Come on, Jenny," he said, poking her with his elbow. "Cheer up. You won't go to hell for this."

She glanced at him. "Oh, I'm not worried about that," she said. "You're the one who needs to worry. The Lord does not bless those who lead the innocent away from the path of righteousness," she intoned. "Have you looked into the depths of your soul?" she asked, fixing a solemn eye on him.

Suddenly his face melted into a smile and she blushed. What is happening to us? Jenny wondered, feeling the tightening inside of her. Whatever it is, I don't want it to stop.

"We're next," Charley said, pulling her up by the hand.

The zoo was crowded with Sunday-morning families, the iron fences covered with pointing, eager children and distracted parents. Charley and Jenny wandered slowly through, stopping occasionally to point something out to each other. They both knew the zoo well from trips there as children with Pa leading the way on his bicycle. On the way out, they bought some popcorn and fed part of it to the ducks who swam through their murky water in lazy circles.

"The zoo depresses me," Jenny said as they started home. "All those sad, dirty animals locked up all day. Think of waking up to that life every morning."

"Anthropomorphist," Charley said.

"All right, smarty, what does that mean?"

"Same thing as fish thinking. Attributing human emotions to animals." He kicked at a stone and missed. "But I agree with you this time. I felt that way when we went to the circus last year. All the animals were doing things they weren't made to do. It's weird and unnatural. I wanted them to rise up and rebel."

He really is sort of good-looking, Jenny was thinking. His face has changed this summer. It doesn't look so soft.

"You're actually getting tan," Jenny pointed out. "You don't have that boiled look this summer."

"Why, thank you," Charley said. "That's the most backhanded compliment I've ever heard." But he was pleased.

Ma didn't say anything to them when they got home. Jenny had a funny feeling that she knew what they had done, but Charley told her it was all in her head.

It was that night after the zoo, Jenny decided later, although exact times began to get mixed up in her mind. She just always thought of it as the dividing night. On that night, the summer cracked and fell into two parts in her mind.

She was lying on her bed reading when someone knocked softly on the door. She knew it was Charley before she opened the door. He had gotten into the habit of coming up to sit with her after dinner. Usually they sat out in the treehouse, but it was raining.

"Come in," she called.

He closed the door quietly behind him and sat down on the end of her bed.

"It's too wet outside?" he asked.

She nodded. "It's pouring. We should build a cover over it." She closed her book and slid down on the bed. Her legs brushed against his foot and she felt suddenly numb. Something is going to happen to us tonight, she realized. He had brought his notebook.

"I wrote the story about Moses over again. Part of it." He put the book down on the bed without opening it. He wasn't ready to read it yet, and she didn't press him. They had gotten used to being silent together. The rain blew in onto the floor, but neither one of them got up to shut the window. Jenny leaned her head back against the wall and watched Charley, who was drawing designs on the bedspread with his finger. His blond hair had turned almost white in the sun, and when it hung straight down, the longest piece touched the tip of his nose. It must tickle his face all the time, she thought with a smile. She almost asked him if it did, but she didn't want to break up the silence with a silly question. He is feeling the electricity, just the way I am. He must be.

Finally Charley propped his head up on his hand and opened the notebook. He read slowly and carefully.

"Before the dog died, he never knew what she thought. He had been living in his own tight world, filled with the dog and his writing and nothing else. He resented the others. The older brother who would always be the strong, forward one, and the younger sister who tagged along behind him. It was always the two of them, planning and building and changing together. And he was always on the outside, standing at the edge with his hands curled angrily into his pockets and his dog beside him, pretending he didn't care that they hadn't asked him in. Sometimes he caught her looking curiously at him and he would walk away, the dog loping slowly behind him."

Jenny felt the tears starting down her cheeks, but she didn't make a sound. Charley took a deep breath and went on reading without looking up at her.

"But when the dog was shot, she was with him. When she saw him crying and knew that he wanted to stop, she talked to him. When he screamed at her that she didn't understand, that she never would, he realized all at once that she did.

She put her arms around him, and all the anger and loneliness that was inside him was suddenly inside her too."

He shut the book and pushed it onto the floor.

She smiled at him. "It's fine, Charley," she said very slowly, her voice steady but strangely off-key.

He looked at her face. "I didn't mean to make you cry," he said gently.

She couldn't stand it anymore. She put her hands over her face, afraid that all the longing showed in her eyes. "Hold me, Charley," she whispered to her wet palms, but he was already moving toward her. He put his arms around her trembling shoulders and pulled him against her. She pressed her face against his chest, smelling the clean cotton of his shirt and the damp skin beneath. He was kissing the top of her head and whispering to her. "Oh, Jenny, God." They rocked gently together, his hand sliding over and over again down the smooth length of her hair. The trembling finally stopped, but they hung on to each other for a long time. Finally he pulled gently away and lowered her onto the pillow. She did not open her eyes until she heard the door close softly behind him.

He stopped on the landing and listened to the sounds downstairs. His parents were talking quietly in the living room. He slipped past them and went out onto the front porch.

The rain had stopped, and on the street some kids were still riding their bicycles up and down the hill in the dark. He smiled, remembering the way they used to beg Ma to let them stay out just a little longer. He thought of Jenny.

He had never felt so close to someone before. He smiled, thinking of the way they could say something without even speaking. Who would ever think that this could happen to two people in so little time? He leaned over the iron railing and looked down toward the hole. He didn't want to stop what was happening to them, but in the last hour things had changed. "God, it feels good to hold a girl like that," he whispered. "But she's my sister."

He turned quickly and went inside.

Chapter Eight

Jenny didn't want it to stop. She lay on her bed in the hot full afternoons, reliving the moment of that holding, feeling again the tickle all over her body as he had rocked her gently back and forth. She was sure it was wrong, but for once she didn't care. She just wanted to feel it again, and there was a difference now when she and Charley were together. Although they never talked about it, the electricity was there, stronger than ever.

They worked even harder on the hole. Charley said he wanted to be sure it was finished by the time John got home, but he knew too that he liked being close to Jenny. Often he caught himself watching the way she moved as she bent over the shovel or lifted the bucket up to him. And he was also remembering the perfect rhythm of that hug.

"Do you think we've gone down deep enough now, Charley?" Jenny called one afternoon early in August.

His face appeared at the edge of the hole. "Let's measure it again," he said.

Jenny took the yardstick from him and laid it against the wall, moving slowly up the ladder.

"Thirteen feet," she said triumphantly when she reached the top. "That's got to be deep enough."

He nodded. "Okay, let's start making the room."

"It makes me nervous," she admitted, staring back down into the hole. "That earth must be incredibly heavy. How do we know it's not going to suddenly cave in on us?"

"John said the composition of the clay makes it hold together—" he frowned. "Or something like that."

"Do you think we should ask Pa?"

Charley considered the suggestion for a minute. "He might not let us go on with it," he said.

"He was out here yesterday looking around. If he hasn't stopped us yet, I don't think he'll say anything now."

"All right," Charley said. "Let's start the room today and we'll ask him tonight. You come out now and I'll start digging again."

They changed places. As she hooked up the buckets, Jenny realized how much longer Charley was able to dig now. He hadn't had asthma for a couple of weeks.

Pa seemed pleased that they were asking his advice. He walked around the edge of the hole for a while.

"I came out and looked at it yesterday," he admitted. "You two have really put in some work on this."

"Climb down the ladder, Pa," Jenny said. When he had reached the bottom, she and Charley leaned over the edge.

"You see, we want to build the room in toward the hillside," Charley explained. "We thought it would be safer that way."

"Hand me down one of the shovels," he said. He poked around for a minute. "It is very heavy soil. I think you'd be better off putting in some supports."

"How do we do that?" Jenny asked.

"You start building the room, and then you run some two-by-fours in through the roof of it. I could help you do it if you want. We'd have to figure out a way of attaching them." He was silent for a minute. "I think it would be best to put some supporting posts up the side, too." He crawled back up the ladder. "Ma probably has some of the lumber we need in her workshop. We could ask her."

"You mean once we dig it out, we'd actually build a little room in there?" Jenny asked.

Pa nodded. "We'd better make a cover for the hole. I don't want some little kid to wander by and fall in. I must admit you two have gone a lot farther with this than I ever thought you would. It was John's idea originally, wasn't it?"

"His idea and our muscles," Jenny said with a frown.

"What are you going to do when he gets back?" Pa asked.

"What do you mean?"

"Doesn't he consider it his hole?"

"We'll take care of him," Charley said quickly. Pa looked at him for a minute."

"Let's go look for the lumber," Jenny said. She turned away. The way Charley said "we" made her smile. In so little time, so much had changed.

"Pa's really gotten involved," Jenny said to Charley that night after dinner.

They were walking down the driveway. Charley had avoided the treehouse ever since that night. He was scared of what might happen between them. They were walking such a tightrope already, and the tension it was building up inside of him was beginning to drive him crazy.

"I wonder if Pa's surprised at me," Charley said slowly. "After all, I've never gotten mixed up in your projects before."

"Are you still mad at him, Charley? About Moses?"

Charley shrugged without saying anything. Although he still thought about that morning, he felt now as if it had happened years ago.

"I guess I'm sort of confused about it. I see now that there was nothing Pa really could have done then," he said, thinking out loud. "But something about him really bothers me. He plays such games. It's so hard for him to come out and be straight with us."

"It's all part of that stiff-upper-lip, don't-show-emotion thing that he and Ma are in," Jenny said. "You know, the way they never let us see them show affection toward each other."

"We've always just accepted the way they are. We've never demanded more. I wonder what would happen if one of us suddenly hugged Pa or burst into tears at the table or screamed at them. Even John's rebellion is controlled."

They stopped at the end of the driveway and watched two kids coming down the hill on their bikes, no hands, their mouths open and screaming.

Charley smiled. "I remember when we used to do that."

Jenny was listening to the birds. This time of the evening

the whole woods seemed to ring with their calls and trills and shrieks.

"Listen to that," she said softly. "It sounds so rehearsed. First the cardinal, then the pip-pip-squeak, then that crow, then the same ones over again in the same order."

Charley laughed. "The evening concert."

"Let's go around the block," Jenny said. "Up through the school playground."

"Okay."

Lately she had begun to feel an impending sense of everything ending. It was already August, and soon Lucy would be home. Then John and then school. How would all that change the way she and Charley had become? She hated to think about it, and she tried to prolong the times they were alone together.

"It's as if Ma and Pa are scared to get too close," Charley said, picking up their earlier conversation. "If they don't look too carefully, they won't see anything."

"You make them sound like two ostriches," Jenny said with a laugh. "I like to think they just trust us. When your kids are as old as we are, you can't go on worrying about every little thing they do. You have to let go sometime."

"But they were never holding on," Charley said.

Jenny looked away.

"The summer really is ending," she said quietly. "Pretty soon Lucy will be home. And then John."

Charley had been thinking of that too. He was looking forward to John's amazement when he saw the hole.

They had reached the back door again. Ma and Pa were out on the front porch.

Jenny looked at Charley's face in the darkness. "Everything will be changing," she said quietly.

He smiled at her. "Let's not think about it now," he said, opening the door. He wanted to say, it's got to change, Jenny. We can't go on like this forever. We're living in a dream world. But he didn't even want to put it into words.

Jenny was down at the bottom of the hole when Lucy phoned. She was surprised at the sinking feeling inside her. "After all, she is my best friend," she muttered, as she climbed up the ladder. But she knew her voice sounded strained when she said hello.

"Can I come over?" Lucy asked. "I can't wait to see this famous hole. That's all you've written me about."

"We spent the whole summer working on it," Jenny said slowly. She was trying to think of an excuse. She knew Lucy would have to come sooner or later, but she wanted to put it off just a little longer.

"My mother said she could drop me off in about an hour."

"Okay," Jenny said in a low voice. "That's fine."

"What's wrong?"

"Oh nothing," Jenny lied. "I'm just tired. I've been working all day."

Charley was climbing up the hill from the stream when she got back.

"Where did you go?" he asked.

"Lucy called. She's coming over," Jenny said shortly, climbing back down the ladder.

"She's home already?" Charley said.

"That's what I was talking about. The summer's almost over."

He looked down at her, caught by the bitter sound of her voice. He crouched down by the ladder and smiled. He wanted to tell her that no matter who came home, there were some things between them that would never change. They stared at each other for a long minute before she bent over her shovel and the time to say anything had passed. Charley stood up. She felt as if her throat were closing.

Jenny heard the car door slam, but she kept on digging.

"Hello," said Lucy's voice.

"Hi, Lucy," Charley said. I've never heard him say her name before, Jenny thought.

"Where's Jenny?"

"Down the hole."

Just as Lucy's head appeared at the edge of the hole, Jenny looked up.

"Hi," Jenny said shyly.

"You digging to China?" Lucy asked with a grin.

"I feel as if we've been there and back."

"This is incredible. Can I come down?"

"Sure. It's still a little tight with two of us down here, but you can fit."

Jenny squeezed herself back into the beginnings of the room so Lucy could stand up straight beside her.

"Aren't you worried that the earth might come crashing down on you?"

"Charley and I spent our whole summer down here. We've gotten used to it."

Lucy started back up the ladder. "What do your parents think of it?"

"They've gotten all involved. Ma's going to saw up the

lumber for the room, and Pa's going to help us put it in. I think they're a little surprised at how far we've gone with this. We want to have the whole thing finished by the time John gets back in about two weeks."

Charley was at the top waiting for them. "What do you think?" he asked eagerly.

Lucy smiled. "Very impressive. I didn't know you were planning to spend your summer underground."

He hooked up a bucket, and the three of them stood in silence watching it rocket down between the trees. Lucy jumped when the empty one hit the tree above them.

"The marvels of modern science," she said quietly.

"Let's go up to my room, Lucy," Jenny said.

"Wait a minute," Charley said. "We have to do a lot more digging before we can put the lumber in."

"I'll be back this afternoon," Jenny said, avoiding his eyes.

"Lunch break," Lucy called back at him as they went up the steps to the porch.

"I feel as if I've been freed from prison," Lucy announced as she threw herself down on the bed.

"It was that bad?" Jenny asked.

"Oh, I guess not. I've just been cooped up all summer with a bunch of screaming kids. I can't wait to spend some time with some regular, intelligent, mature people." She grinned. "Like you."

Jenny pushed open the window and leaned against the sill. "How's your mother?"

Lucy shrugged. "Same as ever. Just a little more in love

with her piano teacher. That story about Moses was awful. How is Charley doing?"

"All right," Jenny said.

"He's changed a lot. It always used to be vague Charley off with Moses, scribbling in that notebook. This summer he's all tan and handsome, shoveling dirt and lifting buckets. What's come over him?"

Jenny moved over to the other bed. She didn't want Lucy to watch her face. She was afraid too much would show in her expression.

"When Moses died, it was sort of a release for Charley. I got him interested in digging the hole, because he was just lying around mourning for Moses. I guess all the exercise helped him a lot. He hardly ever gets asthma anymore. John is going to be amazed when he sees how things have changed around here."

Lucy propped herself up on her elbow. "It sounds as if you and Charley got to know each other pretty well this summer. When I left, you were groaning about having to spend the whole time here with him."

"That seems so long ago now," Jenny said quietly. Suddenly she felt like telling Lucy about what had happened. "He read me some of the stuff he's written. He's very good."

"Gosh, I'll have to ask him if I can read some of it," Lucy giggled. "Like that line, 'Hey, Charley, come show me your etchings.' "

Jenny glanced at her. "He's very serious about his writing."

"I was only kidding, Jenny." Lucy flopped over on her back. "But you must admit, Charley is quite the handsome

93

young man these days. You can't keep him locked away in that hole much longer."

Jenny didn't say anything. She was furious, but she knew now she could never tell Lucy why.

"It's time for me to find a man," Lucy said dreamily. "That's why the summer's been so frustrating. I need to be loved," she added dramatically.

"Me too," Jenny said absentmindedly.

"I wish I had a brother for you," Lucy said with a sly smile. She sat up. "Just watch me go into action. You are going to see the seduction of the century."

"I thought you would set your sights higher than Charley," Jenny said in a low voice. "Surely he's not much of a catch."

"Do I detect a note of jealousy, my dear?" Lucy grinned. "Right now, he's the only catch around."

Jenny jumped up. She couldn't stand this conversation any longer. "Let's go out on our bikes. You can use Ma's."

"All right. Won't Charley be mad that you aren't digging?" But Jenny ran down the stairs without answering.

Jenny realized later that she could have talked to Charley about it. She could have warned him. But that night as she lay in bed with the sheets thrown back, she decided it would be a good test. He would have to choose between her and Lucy.

Chapter Nine

When Lucy first offered to help them with the hole, Charley had been pleased. "We have to get it done before John comes home," he reminded Jenny, ignoring the dark look on her face.

"But I thought you hated small, dark places," Jenny said.

"Oh, I won't go down in the hole," Lucy said. "But I can spread the dirt down at the bottom of the hill, and I can help with the buckets."

"I think it's a great idea," Charley said.

"Don't you want me to help?" Lucy asked, looking at Jenny.

"Of course I do," Jenny said quickly. Inside she was screaming no. Go home. I don't want to play this game. Her smile was strained. She couldn't stand the way they were looking at her. "Charley, you start digging, and I'll go down with Lucy and show her where to spread the dirt."

When they had reached the bottom of the hill, Lucy poked her and grinned. "After a while, you and I can switch places. Then Charley and I will be alone."

"Look, Lucy, this little game is all your idea. Charley and I worked damn hard on the hole, and we both want to get it finished before John comes home. That's all I care about right now. So since I obviously have a lot more practice digging than you do, I'll stay at the top of the hill. You'll just have to find some other time to do your flirting." She turned quickly and clambered back up the hill before Lucy could say anything.

"It sounds like you don't really want Lucy to work on the hole," Charley remarked as Jenny hooked up the first bucket. "With her spreading the dirt as it comes down, we can get a lot more done up here."

"Don't get your hopes up," Jenny said wryly. "She's never been able to concentrate too long on any one thing."

Charley went back to work without a word. He was sure he knew what was bothering her, but he didn't want to talk about it.

Jenny turned out to be wrong. Lucy didn't come back up the hill until Charley called to her. Pa had arrived to inspect their progress.

"A new recruit, I see," Pa said, looking at Lucy's dirt-streaked legs. "The hole disease seems to be catching," he added with a smile. "What's your pay?"

"Free admittance at all times," Lucy intoned. "Except Sunday and holidays when the meeting room is reserved for religious observances."

Pa laughed. "Well, I'm glad you're back among us, Lucy. I knew something vital had been missing all summer."

Lucy giggled.

"What about the room, Pa?" Jenny asked impatiently. "Can we start putting the lumber in yet?"

"Almost. Ma wants to do the sawing today. I'll measure the spaces, and then I'll take your place, Jenny, and you can go help your mother with the lumber."

Jenny stomped down the cellar stairs. Suddenly their hole was turning into a community project. She didn't like the way Pa took her place and sent her off on his errands. And Charley just went along with anything.

"You look like the wrath of God this afternoon," Ma said, glancing up at her. "If you come down those stairs any harder, there won't be anything left of them."

Jenny was silent. She didn't know if she wanted to talk to Ma about it.

"What's wrong?" Ma asked, as they fitted the wood into the saw. "Did you and Lucy have a fight?"

"Sort of," Jenny mumbled. "I guess we've both changed over the summer."

"Here goes the saw," Ma warned. The whine of the saw was so loud in the small room that they could only signal to each other when it was running.

"Changed in what way?" Ma continued, as she took the wood out of the vise.

Jenny shrugged. "It's not just Lucy. Suddenly the hole is becoming a big project for everybody to do in their spare time. Charley and I worked on it so hard all summer, and now when the fun part comes, everybody wants to pitch in."

"You'd rather not have us put the lumber in?" Ma asked. "Pa was just worried that the earth might cave in without some support."

"Oh, I don't know what I want," Jenny exploded. I want Lucy to go back to her camp, she admitted to herself. It would have been all right with just Ma and Pa. Ma was watching her.

"Come on, let's finish the rest of the sawing," Jenny said. "Pa thinks we can put it in this evening. I'm just exasperated by everything today."

They didn't say anything more. Don't probe, Ma, Jenny thought as they were carrying the wood out through the garage. You never know what you might find out.

One afternoon later that week, Jenny left. She couldn't stand it any longer. Charley seemed to spend most of his time going down the hill to check on the bucket rope or to see if Lucy was still working. And Lucy was looking very pleased with herself.

"The hell with it," Jenny muttered, as she hooked up the third bucket in a row. "The hell with them, the hell with this hole. I hope it caves in." She threw her shovel down and climbed over the wall. Charley saw her bicycle disappearing down the driveway as he clambered back up the hill. He called to her once, but when she didn't stop, he gave up.

Let her go. Lucy can help me with the buckets, he thought. He yelled down to Lucy.

"What's wrong?" she asked, when she reached the top.

"Jenny took off and I need someone to hook up the buckets," Charley said quickly as he came down the ladder.

"Where did she go?"

"I don't know. She just took off on her bike."

They worked for a while in silence. The lumber lay in a

pile beside the hole. Pa had fit in two posts, but he decided they had to finish digging out the whole room before they could shore it up any more.

"All right, here's another bucket," Charley called. Lucy was sitting on the wall. She took it from him and sent it banging down the hill.

"Let's take a rest," she said quietly. "It's boiling."

"One more bucket," Charley said, leaning over the shovel again. He felt like stopping too, but he knew Jenny would be mad. She was mad at him no matter what he did these days. He realized that as long as Lucy was around, she was going to act this way. And he was enjoying Lucy. She had always just been Jenny's friend before. Now, suddenly, she was a girl who seemed to like being with him. He was flattered and intrigued.

"All right," he said, as they watched that bucket bang down the hill. They hoisted themselves up on the wall and took long drinks of lemonade from the thermos. Charley felt suddenly shy and clumsy. When you are working away at something, the silences are comfortable, he decided. But now we have to talk to each other.

"Ugh," Lucy said, when she handed him back the thermos. "I drank too much. I feel bloated."

What can I say to that? Charley asked himself. I know what you mean. I feel bloated too. He grinned.

"What are you smiling at?" Lucy asked, looking self-conscious.

"I was trying to invent some small talk about feeling bloated. I feel bloated too. Isn't it an awful feeling? Oh, how I hate to feel bloated."

She laughed. Some other girl might have thought I was making fun of her, Charley thought.

"Why can't people just be silent with each other if they don't have anything to say?" Lucy asked.

"Because we've been told that it's rude."

"Isn't that ridiculous? I think small talk about nothing is even ruder and a big waste of time. If I don't have anything interesting to say to you, I won't say anything."

"Okay. Same here. We'll just sit on this wall like two zombies."

They sat. Charley banged his heels against the cool brick. Lucy pulled her knees up to her chin and stared at the hole.

"Tell me what happened with Moses," she asked quietly. "Jenny just wrote me something about him being shot."

Charley was silent for a long time. It startled him to have her ask that. He realized he hadn't thought about Moses much lately.

"A farmer shot him. He was chasing the man's chickens early one morning. I think about five of them dropped dead from exhaustion, so the man shot Moses. He carried him across the field and dropped him at Pa's feet." He took a deep breath. "It was awful."

"What did your father do?"

"Nothing really. I was furious at Pa in the beginning, but now I realize there was nothing he could do. It was too late. Moses was already dead. That man was really sort of crazy, I think." Charley smiled. Things between Pa and him had changed. Pa seemed genuinely proud of the way he had stuck to it on the hole.

"Funny about this hole," Lucy said after a while. "Everybody's got a different reason for working on it."

"What do you mean?"

"Well, as I see it, Jenny is digging this hole because she started it. She has this mania about finishing things. Your parents have joined in because your father is an architect and got excited about it, and your mother has the lumber and the saw and knows how to use them."

"What about me?" Charley asked.

"I don't know," she said, glancing quickly at him. "To prove something, I guess, but I don't know what."

"After Moses was killed, I didn't want to do anything, but Jenny got me involved in this. She was trying to help me forget. And after all, once you've gone down five feet, it is stupid just to leave it. It sort of became a way of life for me and Jenny. Our whole summer has revolved around it."

"John is going to be surprised," Lucy said.

"He sure is," Charley said with a smile. "I can't wait to see his face."

"So you're really trying to prove something to John?"

"I guess so." He looked at her. "Why are you so wrapped up in this project?"

She didn't answer.

"Are you thinking or are you refusing to answer?" he asked.

"It's one of your more imaginative projects," she said quickly. "Building a treehouse is ordinary, run of the mill. This has a certain flash of originality to it."

He didn't press her, but he was sure she wasn't telling the whole truth. "She really just wants to be near me," he said out loud in his room that night. Then he laughed at himself. The idea pleased him. He lay on his bed, thinking about Lucy and the way she looked, curled up on that wall with her chin resting on her knees. He liked the way her hair curled just at the edge of her shoulder. He imagined himself reaching out to stroke it and letting his arm slip around her shoulders. He knew what it would feel like to hold her. "That's why I let it happen with Jenny," he whispered. "I wanted to see what it would be like to hold a girl like that." But even as he said it, he knew there had been more to that hug.

The bike ride was good for Jenny. It had been months since she had ridden that far from home, and her legs ached as she climbed the cellar steps. The house was empty. She crept into Pa's office and closed the door quietly behind her.

The springs in the sofa were broken, and the big red cushions seemed to swallow her up when she sank down. With her head propped up on the arm, she could just see the bird feeder swinging back and forth from the bounce of a hungry squirrel.

The office had become her thinking place. Pa would come home from work and find her curled up in the couch, staring out the window. Sometimes they would talk, but often he would sit down quietly at his desk and work. The silences are as comfortable as the talks, Jenny decided.

This time she was thinking about Lucy. Getting away from the house and the hole for the afternoon had loosened her up. She decided she could enjoy both Charley and Lucy without getting so wrapped up in them. And John was coming home soon. Maybe he would have changed over the summer. Maybe things would be back to normal between them. She smiled and turned over on her side. When Pa came in, she was asleep.

But the anger came back again when she walked out on the porch and saw them sitting side by side on the wall.

"I leave for one afternoon and the whole thing falls apart," Jenny said as she came up behind them.

Charley scrambled to his feet. "Yes, Master. Right away, Master," he hammed, bowing and backing up until Jenny grabbed his arm because she was scared he might fall off the wall.

"Get down into that hole," she ordered, falling into the game. "And you," she shouted, whirling around and pointing to Lucy. "Back to those buckets. Bring me my whip," she shouted at an imaginary slave.

"We sent down five full buckets," Lucy said.

"Is that all?" Jenny said contemptuously. "Move aside, Charley, and let me in there."

Charley glanced at Lucy. She smiled and waved at him as she slid down the hill to the stream.

He stood there waving back at her until she bent over her shovel at the bottom of the hill. Then he pulled his hand down quickly, scared that Jenny might have seen him. But she was already at the bottom of the hole.

It went along like that. Small signs. Charley could feel himself watching out for her every morning.

"Charley, where are you?" Jenny called from the bottom of the hole. "I've been yelling at you to take this bucket."

He came up to the edge and took the bucket from her. "I've been up on the road," he said quickly. "Lucy's late this morning."

"So what?" Jenny muttered. She looked up.

Charley blushed and turned away. Jenny made him angry

and sad at the same time. Sometimes when she looked at him he felt as if he had betrayed her. But he didn't want to stop what was happening between him and Lucy.

One afternoon he walked home with her.

"Do you want to come up?" Lucy asked, when they got to the front door of her building.

"Okay," Charley said.

Lucy's mother opened the door. She looked startled to see Charley.

"Mother, this is Charley, Jenny's brother," Lucy said quickly, leading him past her into the living room.

"Hello," Mrs. Franklin said, putting her hand up to smooth down her hair. "I didn't realize Jenny had a brother."

"She has two brothers," Lucy said. "I've told you that." She turned to Charley. "My mother never remembers anything except the piece she's playing on the piano. She can sit down and play that through without stopping."

Mrs. Franklin blushed. "Lucy's right. I'm terribly vague. I couldn't get along at all without her."

"Do you want a Coke?" Lucy asked as she walked into the kitchen.

"Sure." Charley glanced around him wondering if he should sit down. Mrs. Franklin was watching him nervously. What a strange woman, he thought.

"Sit down," Lucy called from the kitchen. "Mother, can you come help me bring these in?"

Charley sat down on the edge of a chair. The living room was comfortably furnished, but the low ceilings and white walls made it seem small and cold. The fireplace was surrounded by small blue tiles.

"It doesn't even work," Lucy said, when she saw where he was looking. She handed him a glass and a plate of cookies. "I hate apartments," she said simply. "That's why I spend so much time at your house."

"Lucy keeps telling me we ought to move, but I haven't found a house that I like yet," Mrs. Franklin said as she sat down across from him.

"We haven't really looked, Mother," Lucy reminded her. Charley liked the gentle way Lucy spoke to her mother, but he felt uncomfortable sitting with them. He drank his Coke quickly.

"I was going to do the shopping," Mrs. Franklin said suddenly. "But I'll wait for you to come with me, Lucy." Her voice trailed off.

Charley frowned. He stood up. "I've got to go. Jenny's probably waiting for me."

"Oh, don't go so quickly," Mrs. Franklin said. But Lucy had stood up. She walked with him out to the elevator.

"Sorry about Mother," she whispered. "She's just very nervous around people."

He nodded. The elevator was taking forever.

"She didn't think she ought to leave us alone in the apartment, I guess," Lucy said, thinking out loud. "I never do the shopping with her."

The elevator door opened and he stepped inside. "See you tomorrow," he said. But she had turned away.

Charley walked home quickly, angry with himself for having been so embarrassed. He wondered if Mrs. Franklin really thought they would do something if they were left alone. The idea was ridiculous. He hadn't even kissed Lucy yet.

"Where have you been?" Jenny asked, leaning over the edge of the treehouse.

Charley looked up. "Walking," he said, knowing it sounded lame.

"Where's Lucy?"

"She went home, I guess," Charley lied, starting up the front porch steps.

"You want to do some more work this afternoon?" Jenny asked.

"No, I have to clean out my aquarium. See you later."

Jenny curled up against the trunk of the tree. "Yeah, see you," she said softly.

"Sometimes people just change and grow away from each other," Jenny said to Pa one day. She was standing beside him at the desk, watching him draw.

"Yes," he said, wondering what was coming next.

"And you can't really do anything to stop it, can you? It just happens that way. You just have to accept it."

"That depends. If it's something specific that's bothering you, maybe you can just tell the other person. Talk it out with them," Pa said slowly.

She shook her head. "No, I couldn't do that," she said firmly. "It's not something you can talk out."

"Is it Lucy?" Pa asked gently.

Jenny frowned. She hadn't meant to be specific. "Nobody special. I was just wondering about something," she said quickly, as she went out the door.

They put in the last piece of lumber the week before John came home.

"It almost looks like a house," Charley said reverently. Pa solemnly shook Jenny's hand and then Charley's. "Congratulations, you two," he said quietly. "This is really an achievement." Charley smiled. At last Pa was treating him like the other two. Nobody had mentioned the asthma in months. And I haven't really had any, he realized.

Lucy was still spreading the dirt at the bottom of the hill. She came up when Charley called her.

"The dirt's all spread," she gasped, when she finally reached the top.

"Look at the room," Charley said proudly. Lucy climbed down the ladder and walked all around, running her hands along the wallboards.

"It really is a house, isn't it?" Lucy said.

"That's just what Charley said," Pa pointed out, hoisting himself up on the wall. He was watching Jenny. The tight angry look that he had noticed so often lately had settled onto her face again. It worried him. She saw him looking at her, and she leaned over to pick up her shovel.

When Ma came out on the porch, they called to her. She came down and studied the hole carefully. "Well," she said, after a long silence, "the summer's really over for you two, isn't it?"

"That was a strange thing for her to say, wasn't it?" Charley said to Jenny when they sat together on the wall that evening.

"She's right," Jenny pointed out. "No dirt to dig tomorrow." No reason at all for you to spend any more time with me.

Charley nodded. He was wondering whether Lucy would come over the next day.

"We should have our own celebration," Jenny said slowly, watching his face. "After all, we're the ones who really did this."

He glanced at her. In the evening light, her face was shadowed and indistinct. He felt a sudden warmth again, that mixture of pride and closeness. They had been through a lot together that summer. He didn't want to lose her again.

"Sure," he said, smiling at her. "That's a great idea."

Jenny organized the sleep-out. In her closet she hid John's old sleeping bag, two blankets, some candles she stole from the supply closet, and some food.

Charley looked over the pile approvingly. "I'll bring some wine," he said. "We need something to celebrate with."

She smiled to herself. He really did want it to be something special, just the way she did.

The night was unexpectedly cool. Jenny pulled a sweater on over her shirt before she tiptoed across the hall to wake Charley. He was asleep and she had to shake him twice before he woke up.

"Boy, you were dead to the world," Jenny whispered fiercely. She hadn't been able to fall asleep at all.

They each took a bundle from Jenny's closet and went down the stairs, skipping the fourth step which always creaked.

Jenny pulled the front door shut behind her and stopped a minute on the porch. She took a deep breath of the cool air and listened to the birds. The woods were bursting with their songs, the notes rising over and over again from the dark branches.

Charley went down the ladder first, and Jenny passed him the equipment. He held the flashlight on the ladder as she came down.

"The room looks bigger to me," Jenny said, standing in the middle.

"I was thinking the same thing," Charley said, as he flashed the light into the corners.

They stood in silence, looking around at the place they had built. Charley turned suddenly and grabbed her hand.

"Congratulations," he shouted. "We did this. You and me. Isn't it great?"

She burst out laughing, and they danced around in a tiny circle, the flashlight jerking its light in crazy arcs around the room. Jenny was filled with the warm, trembling feeling that she had nursed and dreamed about. She loved the tight hold Charley had on her hands and the way their bodies balanced each other, leaning out in the circle. And when they finally collapsed on the floor, she let go of him reluctantly.

After a while, she began to crawl around the room, arranging their stores in neat rows. Charley watched her in silence.

"You know it doesn't bother me at all being underground," he said, leaning back on his elbows. "I thought it would."

She lit a candle. Their shadows jumped up and down on the walls.

"I think it might get to me if we didn't have the supports. They do make the place more permanent."

Charley pulled the bottle of wine out of his sack and opened it. He poured them each a glass.

"Here's to us," he said, raising his glass, "and our perseverance and determination."

"And here's to all the afternoons we didn't sneak down to Bartlett Avenue instead," Jenny proclaimed.

"And all the times I didn't clean my aquarium—"

"And all the books on my summer reading list that I didn't read." Jenny giggled and took another swallow of wine.

"And here's to Moses," Charley said somberly. And they both drank slowly. "More wine, waiter," he said, filling both glasses.

Jenny giggled again. The wine made her skin tingle. "Where did you get this bottle, Charley?"

"I found it in the back of the refrigerator." He held the label up to the candle. "It's French, so I figured it couldn't be too bad."

"It's probably Ma's cooking wine."

They lay there in silence for a while, listening to the noise of the trucks on the avenue two blocks away. In between the trucks, they could hear the squirrels and birds settling in the trees.

"A little piece of country, right in the middle of the city," Charley said softly.

Jenny was drifting. Everything was turning out so perfectly, even better than she had imagined. Charley had joined her celebration. It was just the two of them together again, closer than ever before.

He rolled over onto his stomach. "The future," he said solemnly.

She smiled at him. "What?"

"Our game. Things that pop into our minds all the time. Unanswered questions. Have you ever wanted to turn on a television screen and see yourself in ten years? Just catch yourself in the middle of doing something ten years from now."

"I'll be twenty-three," she said. "Ten years might as well be forever." She took another sip of wine.

"After I think about it for a while, I decide that I don't want to know at all. I mean you might turn on the screen one day and it might be blank," he said solemnly.

"It would be so inevitable. Whatever you saw there would just have to be. No way to change it." She shuddered. "I would hate that. It wouldn't be worth living through the ten years."

"You're right."

He lit another candle and handed her a sandwich. She sat up to eat it.

"I like the smell of the wood down here," he said between bites. "It doesn't smell so much like the cellar."

She nodded.

When they had finished eating, she rolled out both blankets, one on top of the other.

"Do you want the sleeping bag?" she asked.

"No, you can have it."

"I'll run it this way so we can both use it as a pillow." She was trembling a little when she curled up on her side of the blankets. It's not because I'm cold, she thought.

"When did you first find out about sex?" Charley asked suddenly, his voice jumping out at her.

Jenny blushed in the darkness. "About the fifth grade, I

guess. From friends at school." She didn't want to tell him it was Lucy. She didn't even want that name to be mentioned. "I bet John told you."

"You're right. I remember he told me some dirty joke I didn't understand, and then he had to explain the whole thing." He laughed nervously. "I almost died."

She smiled. "Same here. On one hand, it seemed so strange, and on the other hand, you felt as if you'd suspected it all along. There was something going on that you'd been left out of."

"I'm glad Ma and Pa didn't tell us," Charley said. "I would have been even more embarrassed."

"Ma tried once with me. She just ended up giving me a book called *You and Your Body* or something like that."

Charley laughed. "Trust them. When something really matters, they just can't bring themselves to talk about it."

Jenny opened her mouth to defend them, but she didn't say anything. She didn't want to disagree with him about anything. Not now. Not when things were like this.

Charley rolled over onto his stomach. "Hey Jenny, do you ever think of them doing it?" His voice was low, almost a whisper. She wanted to reach out and touch him.

"Do you?" he asked again.

"Yes," she said softly. "Sometimes. I can't really believe it."

"Why not? Where do you think we came from?"

"I mean it's because they're our parents. Because they never even hold hands in front of us." She sighed. "Because I've never done it."

"Do you want to?"

She sucked in her breath and held it for a minute. "No," she finally admitted. "I'm scared."

He moved onto his back again and put his hands up under his head. "I can't wait," he said simply.

Then I must be the only one who's scared, she thought. Everybody else is just sitting around waiting to find the right person to make it with. Suddenly she wanted to cry. I just want to be held again, she thought. Feel his hand moving down my hair, over and over again.

Charley was dreaming in darkness. If this were Lucy, he wondered, would I reach out now? Would we make love right here? He heard her moving, and suddenly he felt the warmth of her next to him and the weight of her head on his shoulder. For the longest second, he thought, This is Lucy. She does want me. And he almost put his arm around her and pulled her closer. But the second ended.

"Hey, come on, Jenny, move over," he said, pulling his arm out from under her. "What are you doing?"

She didn't say anything. Her throat was closing up.

When he pulled his arm away, one of the candles fell over. It went out. "Oh, well," he said. "We'd better go to sleep anyway. Do you have enough of the sleeping bag?"

She huddled at her side of the blanket, her legs curled up against her. He flopped back and forth on his side, trying to get comfortable. "These boards are harder than I thought," he said loudly. She still didn't say anything.

"Hey, Jenny," he whispered. "Are you awake?"

"I just wanted to be warm again," she said evenly. "That's all I wanted. I just wanted that time—" She stopped.

"Come on, Jenny. You're my sister. I mean if people even

113

found us down here sleeping beside each other, they might think something was weird." He paused. "That other time, it really shouldn't have happened."

She shivered again. "Oh, shut up, Charley," she said quietly. "I'm trying to get to sleep."

"Ah, shut up, yourself," he said quietly, as if he really didn't mean it. As if he were really saying, I'm sorry.

Chapter Ten

When John came home, Jenny was sitting up in the tree-house. She watched him get out of the car and walk up the steps. He glanced up at the house, but she drew back and he didn't see her.

"I'm not going to say anything to him," she whispered to herself. "Let him come look for me."

Later on she could hear them calling for her, but she didn't answer.

"Jenny, come down, John's home."

"So what," Jenny said softly. She rolled over onto her stomach and hung her head over the edge so she could hear what they were saying on the front porch.

"Charley, do you know where Jenny is?" Ma asked.

"No. Maybe she went out on her bike."

"I feel as if I haven't seen her all week," Ma said slowly.

"It doesn't matter, Ma. I'll talk to her later," John said. He took a glass of lemonade off the tray.

"It doesn't matter to me either, John," Jenny whispered.

"Why don't you show John what you've done on the hole?" Ma said as she went back inside.

I bet that made Charley mad, Jenny thought. He likes to bring things up in his own way.

"You want to look at it now?" Charley asked.

"I had completely forgotten about the hole," John said. "You did some more work on it?"

"We finished it," Charley said proudly. "Come on, I'll show you."

Jenny watched them walk down the steps and across the driveway. Through the leaves, she could only see parts of each of them as they crawled over the wall, but she could still hear their voices.

"Charley, this is amazing," John said slowly. "I never thought you'd get this far."

Charley smiled. "Guess we showed you," he said. His voice was friendly.

"Did you do it all by yourself?"

"No. Jenny and I did it. At the end, Lucy helped us too."

"I can't imagine Lucy at the bottom of this hole," John said, as he climbed down the ladder.

"She came home after camp, and I guess she didn't have anything else to do. She's changed a lot," Charley added.

Jenny inched forward on the platform. They were talking quietly.

"You put in all the lumber too?"

There was a silence.

"Ma and Pa helped," Charley said finally. "We did all the digging, though. But when we started to dig out the hole, we got worried that the earth might collapse on us, so we asked Pa about it."

Jenny held her breath. She was sure John was going to explode.

"Trust them to get involved," he said, as he climbed back up the ladder. "Ma and her saw and Pa and his architecture. It was made for them."

"Are you mad that we let them help us?" Charley asked.

John shrugged. "Who cares, now that it's all done? I can't see either of them wanting to spend much time down here. But with you and me and Jenny and Lucy all sharing it, we're going to have to set up a schedule."

Charley leaned against the wall. "Oh, you can count me out. I spent all summer underground. I need some big open spaces." Funny how he didn't care about the hole anymore. He had just cared about finishing it. About being near Jenny. He took a deep breath and looked off down the hill. John was watching him.

"You seem different," John said shyly. "How was your summer?"

Charley shrugged. "You heard about Moses. That wasn't a great way to start the summer."

"That man sounded crazy."

"I think he was. Well, that's all over now. The summer's gone very quickly." He glanced at John. "I guess we've all changed."

"I think I'll move my stuff in here," John said, staring down into the hole. "It might be fun to spend some nights out here."

117

"Sure. It's comfortable if you bring a blanket. We did it one night."

John shoved his hands in his pockets and turned back up toward the house. "I don't know why I started the hole. I can't even remember."

"And I don't know why we killed ourselves finishing it," Charley said. "I haven't been down here since." Except for that one night. "You should work out a schedule with Jenny, though. She did half the work."

Jenny slid back quietly until her back touched the tree. Yeah, don't forget good old Jenny. She only killed herself digging a hole all summer that nobody wants to use. She felt betrayed, and yet she didn't know why. She never wanted to go down that ladder again either.

Slowly Jenny pulled away from her family. She felt as if she were backing up an aisle and she could see the faces all turning around to stare at her and then she could see the faces growing smaller and smaller. Their mouths were still moving, but she could no longer hear their voices.

Pa watched her and worried. She never came to sit in his office anymore. She spent all day in the treehouse, and when he spoke to her, her eyes looked dazed and unfocused. He mentioned it to Ma.

"I know," she said quietly. "I've noticed it too. I think it has something to do with John. She's feeling left out."

But Pa disagreed. He knew it had all started when Lucy came home.

Jenny watched the family circling her, reaching out to her and drawing back. She laughed to herself.

"Hey, Jenny, can I use your treehouse this afternoon? I

want to see if I can hook up a light for the hole. Ma says I'm using up all her candles."

"Go away, John."

"Please, Jenny. It would only take a little while. I wouldn't bother you."

"No," she shouted. "Just leave me alone."

He slammed the door when he went out. She was braced for it.

Even Charley tried. "Jenny," he shouted up the stairs. "Lucy and I are going down to Bartlett Avenue. You want to come?"

She didn't answer.

"Hey, Jenny?" he called again.

"Leave her alone," Lucy said quietly. "She doesn't want to come with us."

From upstairs, Jenny heard the kitchen door slam. Boy, they tried hard, she muttered. Typical. I don't need any of them anymore. I just need myself. "Just myself," she said out loud, trembling a little at the sound of the words.

They were almost to the fish store before Charley noticed that he hadn't said a word all the way.

"What are you thinking about?" Lucy asked.

He looked up and shrugged.

"Jenny?" she said.

"I don't know why I bother," he answered. "She's acting like a complete baby."

Lucy stepped up onto a low wall and walked along for a while, two heads above him.

"I can see why she's acting that way."

"All right, expert. Why?"

"John's home and she's not getting along with him very well these days. And she had you all to herself all summer before I got home. Now suddenly I spend more time with you than I do with her. And you spend more time with me," she said. She stopped for a minute, wondering whether she should have said that. He was looking down at the sidewalk. "And Jenny doesn't have anybody."

"But we keep asking her to go places with us."

"She doesn't think we really want her. I can see why. You know, three's a crowd."

I don't really want her to come, Charley admitted to himself.

"I remember once when we had a fight at school," Lucy said slowly. "In the car on the way home, we had to sit beside each other, and she got out her notebook and scratched out a whole note I had written her in math class. She was pressing down so hard that her pen went right through the piece of paper. When she gets mad, she's scary." The wall ended and Lucy joined him on the sidewalk again.

Charley wasn't listening. He was thinking about the night in Jenny's room. About the hug. Suddenly he wanted to ask Lucy about it. But it seemed to be the wrong place. Just walking along the street like that.

"Charley, are you still with me?"

He looked at her. "Sorry," he said. "I was thinking."

"Why don't you think out loud?"

"It's not really the right place."

She looked around. "There's nobody near us. We can talk quietly." She was startled by the hard way he was staring at her. As if the look on her face could tell him something.

"It's something that happened between me and Jenny this summer. It must be what's bugging her."

"Okay, what was it?"

"She'd kill me if I told you."

"I won't tell her."

"Well, after we started working on the hole every day, Jenny and I spent a lot of time together. At night we used to sit up in the treehouse and talk about things. I read her a story I wrote about Moses. Then later in the summer, I wrote it over and I read it to her again. We were sitting on her bed and she started to cry—" He stopped.

Lucy was still looking at him. She smiled, encouraging him to go on.

"So I hugged her," he said quickly. "I was just trying to make her feel better. But she kind of made something out of it, I think. I mean she didn't chase after me or anything, but she changed."

Lucy didn't say anything. She was thinking about her talk with Jenny about how good-looking Charley was. That hard look that had settled on Jenny's face.

"Then another time she tried something else," Charley said. "I pushed her away. That made her angry. We haven't really talked since then."

Lucy was watching the sidewalk cracks as they passed underneath her. She was trying to puzzle out something he'd said in the beginning.

"Do you think I was wrong?"

"About hugging her or pushing her away?" Lucy asked.

"Either. Both. The whole thing." He looked at his shoes. "I mean, what do you think?"

"I don't think you guys are weird, if that's what you're

worried about. But I don't think you're really being fair to Jenny."

"What do you mean?" he asked.

"You say you only hugged her because you wanted to make *her* feel better." Charley nodded. Lucy paused, trying to figure out how to say what she meant. "There wasn't anything else to it? I mean, you didn't do it because you wanted to, because you enjoyed it too?" She took a deep breath. There, it was out.

Charley was stunned. She had just asked him the question he had been afraid to answer all summer. The feelings about that hug that he had pushed out of his mind.

He didn't say anything for so long that she wondered whether he was going to answer the question. She couldn't see his face.

"God, Lucy," he said quietly. "You don't leave anything out, do you?"

She blushed. "Never mind. I don't have to know. I just had to ask the question."

"You're right. It was that, too. It feels good to hold a girl like that." He grinned. "But now that's all behind me. Now I've got someone else."

She laughed. They heard bells in the distance. She grabbed his hand and started pulling him off down the street. "The Good Humor man, Charley. Come on," she shouted.

Charley felt as if a cold wave had broken over him, and he kept trying to catch his breath as she pulled him along.

Jenny nursed the angry hard knot inside her. She found reasons to do things she would never have done before. People lie to you when they look at your face, she thought.

You have to spy on them to hear what they really think. She crept around the edges of the family, listening to conversations through windows and half-open doors. The house walled her out, and she hated the house.

She figured out that she could jump from the treehouse to the roof. She had never dared try it before, but suddenly she felt reckless. Once she slipped because she didn't take a running start, but she never made that mistake again. You slip, you fall, people come running.

She took to wandering all over the roof of the house, looking at the trees from even higher up, even farther away. And she listened.

"It wasn't that great a summer," John said, rolling over onto his stomach on the bed. "Andrew got to be kind of a drag. He was always arguing with his father. About everything."

Charley smiled and John caught it. "What are you smiling about?"

"Sounds familiar," Charley said.

"I guess so. But the strange thing was his father never argued back. He just couldn't have cared less what we thought or did or said. They let Andrew do anything he wants. So all the time Andrew is trying to do something more incredible just to get a rise out of them." John shrugged. "It gets boring. At least Ma and Pa give a damn."

Outside Jenny pulled herself closer to the wall. John sure had changed. Inside she felt herself slipping a little. It would be nice to have a talk with him. She shook her head. He hadn't come looking for her. Not once since he'd been home.

"Jenny and I figured out a lot of things about Ma and Pa over the summer," Charley said slowly. "I think they really love us and all that, but they are so scared to show their emotions. They never kiss each other or hold hands. Same with us. Ma hasn't kissed me since I was about six."

"So what? I don't want them walking around, slobbering over us all the time."

"There is a middle road," Charley said sarcastically. "It's so hard for them to talk to us about things, too. They just kind of close their eyes and hope the problem will go away before they have to deal with it."

John sat up. "There are lots of other ways of showing people you love them. We know Ma and Pa love us and each other without everybody having to talk about it all the time. The family all hangs together pretty well. I mean, I'd be really sad if you fell off a cliff or Jenny drowned or something."

"Gee, thanks," Charley said.

John ignored the sarcasm in his voice. "And maybe they trust us to figure out our problems by ourselves. I mean, parents have to let go sometimes."

"Somebody's going to have to get Jenny through this one," Charley muttered. "I don't think she's going to get out of this mood by herself."

"What's eating at her?" John asked. "She comes down to dinner looking like a zombie. I never see her. She hasn't been down to the hole once."

"I don't know," Charley lied. "She was fine all summer. Then something started bugging her."

"How long have you been going around with Lucy?"

"She came home around the middle of August."

"I bet that's what's bugging Jenny," John said. "Sometimes girls are funny about their brothers."

Jenny looked out over the trees. Charley wasn't going to answer that one. Jenny slipped a little as she crawled back to her room, but nobody came to look out the window.

She spent one whole afternoon cleaning up the dollhouse in the cellar. When every tiny piece of furniture had been taken out and dusted, she put them all back, rearranging every room. Wouldn't it be nice if you could change people around that easily, she thought. Rearrange them so they fit together smoothly, so nobody fights or rubs someone else the wrong way. Dust them off and polish them up when they get boring. Fold them up and put them away when you don't want to see them anymore.

"Now, John, I'm afraid we're just a little sick of you this month. So you'll have to stay down in the cellar until you start acting normal again. And Ma, if you keep kicking Pa that way, we'll have to move you to the other side of the living room. If you two are going to act like children, we'll just have to treat you like children." She giggled at the thought. "And Charley, this month we'll just have to fold you up and put you away. Why, that's the third time you've tried to hold Jenny's hand, and you know what we think about that." She stopped. She hated this house, too, just as much as the one she was sitting in. When she slammed its front door, the little doorknob came off in her hand.

"I thought I heard someone else down here," Ma said, poking her head in the door.

Jenny sat up, closing her hand over the doorknob.

"That really is a lovely old dollhouse Pa gave you. I'm glad you decided to clean it out."

Jenny started to pick up the cleaning rags and the bucket.

"Oh, don't leave, Jenny. I didn't mean to bother you," Ma said quickly.

Ma almost ran away, Jenny thought, as she slipped the doorknob into the pocket of her pants. Everybody's getting a little scared of me, she said with a smile. Except Pa, she remembered. He's just worried.

Pa had come looking for her the night before. After dinner when the family usually gathered on the front porch, Jenny had slipped back up the stairs to the treehouse. When someone knocked on her door, she began to shiver a little, wondering if it was Charley. But she didn't say anything. Pa opened the door slowly and walked in. He sat down on the windowsill behind her, but she didn't turn around, pretending she hadn't heard.

"We miss you downstairs, Jenny. Don't you want to come down and sit on the porch with us?"

Jenny didn't answer. It was scary to keep quiet like that, but she didn't trust herself.

"Ma tells me you cleaned out the dollhouse this afternoon. I went down and looked at it. The doorknob's come off the front door. I thought I would put it back on but I couldn't find it. Do you have it?"

She shook her head. There was a silence. Down below they could hear Charley and John arguing about something. Pa leaned out the window and watched them.

"You really can see everything from up here, can't you?" he said slowly. Jenny nodded. He reached out and patted her arm.

"I miss seeing you," he said simply. And then he was gone.

126

She pulled her knees up to her chin and stared at the one streetlight she could see through the trees. She missed him too, she admitted. He was the one person she was really missing.

It seemed to her that the summer had already turned into fall. The days were filled with that dead, ending feeling that she dreaded so much. The sound of the crickets rose all around her, and the lights from the porch shone on the underside of the leaves. She felt as if she lived all alone in a silvery green house. The talk drifted up, and she listened to the voices the way she would to voices in a dream.

Sometimes she would pull herself closer to the edge and look down at them. They don't even miss me, she thought. They aren't even wondering where I am. Once Charley turned suddenly and looked right up at her. She froze in position, but he didn't wave or say anything. It was just as if he wanted to be sure of something.

One evening when Ma and Pa were alone on the porch, the conversation tuned in clearly. She lay on her stomach, her chin on her hands, watching them and listening. They were talking about John.

"He changed this summer," Ma said. "The tension and anger are gone. He's accepted us for what we are."

"And himself," Pa said, propping his feet up on the iron railing. "He's no longer fighting with himself."

"But we have a new problem," Ma said. "Jenny."

Pa nodded without saying anything. He knows I'm up here, Jenny thought. He knows I can hear them. She slid back a little from the edge.

"She and Charley had such a good time this summer, and now suddenly she's not speaking to anybody. That cold look on her face scares me," Ma said softly.

Pa reached over and touched Ma's arm. They looked at each other for a long time. Ma didn't look up at the tree-house, but she didn't say anything more.

I wish I could be back with them, Jenny admitted as she rolled back toward the tree. She was disappointed with herself for the thought. But I can't just go back to my old self now. Not after what's happened. Not after what Charley thinks of me.

"I feel as if Ma and Pa and I have some wall between us," Charley said to Lucy one morning. "We're all worrying about Jenny, and we see it in each other's faces and we never say a word about it."

"What is there to say?" Lucy asked, feeling around in the back of a drawer. They were down in the cellar. Charley was looking for some wire John had asked him to drop off at the hole. "She's putting on a big act, and I'm getting a little tired of it."

"It's not all an act," Charley said, turning on her. "Jenny's hurt and—and all mixed up. She really needs someone to help her."

"Well, Doctor, what are you waiting for?" Lucy asked. "You're the root of the problem, after all."

He glared at her for a minute and turned away. "I've got the wire," he said sharply. "Let's go."

As they were climbing the stairs, Charley stopped and looked around.

"What's wrong?"

"I thought I heard something," he said quietly. "Never mind."

As they shut the door, Jenny came out from under the stairs and stood looking up into the darkness. She smiled to herself.

"You were hiding under the stairs that day, weren't you?" Charley asked her much later.

"Yes," she admitted. "I followed you around a lot. You never knew it."

He smiled. "Most of the time I knew it," he said.

Jenny realized later that that lonely time at the end of the summer had gone dragging on for weeks. She slipped and hid around the house like a ghost, too scared to run away, too ashamed to be herself again. But things began to change after a while. Her mind kept wanting to think about one certain thing, and after a while, she didn't try to stop it anymore. She would lie on her bed and let her mind nibble at the edges of the thing. The truth of the whole summer. What had really happened and how different she was because of it. And when she had thought for a while and was getting into it too deeply, she'd jump up and wander around the house again, always by herself, avoiding the noisy places where the family sat and talked and laughed and argued.

Then one night she thought it all the way through because she just couldn't stop herself anymore. She lay on the roof, her cheek caught on the smooth, cool slates. Something has to happen soon, she thought. They aren't going to let me go on like this much longer. Ma will talk to Charley about me, and he'll tell her everything. He'll make it sound like I tried to make him do it.

I could just go downstairs to breakfast and be good old Jenny all over again. But as soon as I saw Charley and Lucy whispering together and holding hands—she shuddered. I hate them, she thought, knowing it wasn't true, knowing it was really something inside herself that she hated. Charley has Lucy now. He doesn't need me anymore. But I don't have anyone else. I probably never will.

I wonder if they've slept together. Where could they do it? She lay there, picturing their pitching bodies in a bed. She felt guilty because she was enjoying thinking about it. In the hole, she said to herself suddenly. Of course. She scrambled back along the roof to her window.

John was on the phone in the hall, and he glanced at her curiously when she opened the front door, but he said nothing. She slipped outside and crossed the driveway.

"Charley?" she called softly, half expecting to see his face rise up the ladder. But nobody was there.

She crawled down the ladder and lit one of the candles. John had moved in. She could see his blanket stretched out and a pile of magazines heaped in the corner. The place smelled faintly of smoke and incense. She felt out of place. The hole belonged to John. It always had. Only the making of it had been hers and Charley's. It had given them an excuse to spend so much time together. And now she couldn't even look at him anymore.

She shivered, remembering why she had come down there and what had happened the last time she had been in the hole. "I'm sick," she whispered. "I'm very very sick." She

130

blew out the candle and crawled back up the ladder.

The priests heard confessions on Saturday afternoons. Jenny slipped in the side door and sat down in a pew in the back. The church smelled of smooth wood and incense. She knelt down and leaned her forehead against her arms. Her heart was pounding in her ears, and she held her breath for a minute, trying to make it calm down. "Bless me, Father, for I have sinned," she practiced. "It has been three months since my last confession." How was she going to say it? She lifted her head and stared at the cross over the altar. The crucifix in this church had always bothered Jenny. The figure was made of stone, a cold, smooth Jesus standing in front of his cross. He didn't look sad or hurt, he looked angry and distant. She closed her eyes and tried to pray.

All around the edges of the church, people were leaning in lines against the walls. She heard faint whisperings and then the low-spoken advice of the priests. She stood up and joined the shortest line.

As the line moved forward toward the wooden door covered in black cloth, she kept trying to organize her words. But every time she tried to think about how she was going to say the thing she had come to say, her mouth just started at the beginning again, "Bless me, Father . . ."

The woman in front of her left the door standing open. Jenny walked in slowly and pulled the door closed behind her. She knelt in front of the black screen and squeezed her hands together until they shook. Then the sliding window was pushed back and she could make out the dark shadow of the priest's face.

She leaned forward. "Bless me, Father, for I have sinned.

It has been three months since my last confession." She stopped.

"Yes, my child. Go on." He sounded impatient. He's probably thinking of all the people standing in lines out there. He probably peeks out through the black cloth in between confessions.

"I lied to my parents. I skipped Mass. I said mean things about my friend." She stopped again.

"Is that all?"

"No, Father. I—I had strange feelings about my brother."

"What do you mean? Did you want to hurt him?"

Suddenly she knew this was crazy, this secret huddled whispering about her sins. What this priest said and did over her would not take away that heavy sick feeling inside of her. She stood up slowly and whispered a crazy good-bye to the dark shape. She ran all the way home, her hands pressed against her cheeks, holding her face together. And later, when she lay curled up on her bed, she felt the hot marks her palms had made on her face. She wanted to cry so badly, but the mean ball inside of her would not burst.

Pa came to see her again that afternoon. He stood at the door and looked down on her huddled in the bed.

"Jenny."

Her body went rigid. "What?" she said angrily.

The tone of her voice stopped him for a minute. She realized that and it scared her. Maybe he's going to hit me, she thought, as she rolled over and looked at his face. He looked sad and hurt. She closed her eyes.

"I just wanted to see if I could talk to you about it. Whatever's bothering you, I'm sure it's not as bad as you think it is. If you could just talk it out with someone." He spoke very slowly, as if he had rehearsed the speech.

Pa's not playing games, she thought. He really does want to help. But nobody can take away this dirty feeling inside me. The way I reached out for him. The way I thought about him. She trembled.

"Please, go away, Pa. I don't want to talk to you about it."

The next time she looked up, he was gone. First Charley, now Pa. I spent all summer reaching out to people, and in so little time I've cut them off again.

Charley couldn't sleep. He turned over on his back and lay with his arms thrown out, staring at the ceiling. The aquarium in the corner sent out a constant bubbling noise that he barely noticed anymore.

He was thinking about Jenny. At dinner, she had stared across the table at him with a dazed, bitter look in her eyes. Something had happened to her. She seemed to have turned some crazy corner of her own. John had tried to tease her out of her silence.

"There seems to be a ghost at our table," he said, clanking his fork against his plate. "Tell us what you want, disturbed spirit, and leave us be."

Jenny looked down at her plate. Charley watched her face. Her expression did not change.

"John." Ma was warning him not to go on, but John ignored her.

"Have you lost some passionate lover in these halls? Do you seek to see his face again?" he intoned in a solemn voice.

"Shut up, John," Pa said sharply, startled by the blank

look on his daughter's face. He wished she would fight back or scream or cry. Anything was better than this stretched silence.

"Maybe she needs a spanking," John said quietly. "Nothing else seems to be getting through to her."

Jenny looked across the table at Charley. At first she seemed to be reaching out to him, but then her face suddenly changed. The muscles around her mouth tightened, and she glared at him angrily.

"Jenny?" Ma said tentatively.

She stood up slowly and walked out of the room.

"Jenny," Ma raised her voice. "Jenny, come back here, please." Ma stood up as if to follow her, but she didn't move. The family sat in silence and listened to the bedroom door close quietly and the lock slide across into place.

"She's really gone nutty," John said softly, looking across at the empty chair.

"Oh, John, please be quiet," Pa said. He glanced at Ma, who was still standing at her place looking out the door.

"Charley, I'd like to speak to you alone, please," Ma said, as she walked out of the room.

Even before she said anything, Charley knew what she wanted.

"I want you to talk to her," Ma said, sitting down in a chair in the living room. "Something has happened between you two. Something you've done is bothering her."

"But, Ma—"

"I don't want to know what it is, Charley. But I want you to talk to her."

"Have you tried talking to her, Ma? You and Pa just look the other way and hope we'll work out our own problems.

You can't do that with Jenny this time. She really needs help." He stopped, surprised by the things he was saying. Ma was staring at him. Neither of them said anything for a minute.

"If you could just try, Charley," she begged softly.

She's scared, Charley realized suddenly. She's really scared to get too close.

"She needs someone to hold her," Charley said slowly. "I'm not the right person. I shouldn't be the one to do that."

Ma said nothing.

He stood up. "I'll try, Ma. But you're going to have to do it sometime. We're all waiting for you." He walked out of the room without looking at her again.

He sat up in bed. If I don't do it and get it over with, I won't ever have the nerve. The hall light was still on, and he flicked it off as he padded across to her room. He didn't want the light to wake her when he opened the door.

Jenny opened her eyes. Something was wrong. There was somebody in the room with her. She could hear the breathing, and she could make out the faint lines of the body. She shut her eyes again and turned as if in her sleep. When she looked again, she could see that it was Charley. He was standing there, staring down at her. She felt her heart pounding in her throat.

"Jenny," he said quietly. "Jenny, are you awake?"

"Get out of here," she warned. Her voice was trembling. "Get out before I scream."

"Wait a minute, Jenny. I want to talk to you." He lowered himself onto the bed so that she could feel the warmth and the bulk of his body through the sheets.

She screamed. It was a long, high-pitched scream that flew in and out of the corners of the room until it finally ended in the ragged crying that had been building up inside of her for so long.

Chapter Eleven

Someone was holding Jenny. She let herself be rocked back and forth on the bed like a baby. Her mother was whispering to her, little nonsense words, little comforts from the days of scraped knees and bruises. She felt her hair smoothed away from her wet cheeks.

"I'm all right now, Ma. I'm just tired." She pushed gently away and lay down on the pillow.

"I'm right down the hall if you want me," her mother whispered as she tucked in the sheets. "We won't talk about it tonight. You can tell me tomorrow if you want to."

Jenny nodded without saying anything. She closed her eyes until she heard the door softly close.

Something had burst inside her, and she felt tired and drained, as if a great wave had rolled her over. All the hate and anger were gone. Now she wanted to tell somebody.

He had been there. She had seen his worried face in the

background, watching her and waiting. He had been waiting ever since the mean thing inside of her had started to grow. She would tell him tomorrow.

She watched the afternoon sun slip across the drawings spread on her father's desk. The bars between the window-panes made dark crosses on the white paper. She heard Charley come down the stairs two at a time. He went out on the porch and stood at the railing, looking down into the woods. She was watching him through the window, but he didn't look around at her. After a while, he turned and ran down the porch steps.

Outside in the branches the squirrels chattered and spat, their gray tails jerking and curling against them. She watched them idly, smiling at their fussing.

The back door slammed. Pa was home. She curled back farther into the corner of the couch and watched the door. He stopped in the kitchen and said something in a low voice to Ma. Then she heard his footsteps approaching.

When he opened the door, he glanced first at the couch. As if he had looked there before, she thought later. As if he hoped she would be waiting for him. He smiled when he saw her and closed the door softly behind him.

When she saw him smile, she felt suddenly like crying. He had been waiting for her to come and now she was there. She was scared of what he would say, but she knew she had to tell him everything. This was her confessional.

He sat down beside her. "You've had quite a time, haven't you?" he asked.

"I came to tell you about it," she said softly. "I've been waiting here all afternoon."

138

He settled back into the couch.

"But I'm not quite ready," she said. "I have to think it out a little more."

He nodded without saying anything. In the silence between them, the noises of the house came into focus again. From the cellar they could hear the muffled banging of the hammer. Pa smiled at the sound.

"Your mother can take out all her worries pounding away down in that cellar," he said.

Jenny nodded without saying anything. She had wanted to talk to Ma but she couldn't. Not yet.

"She's very worried about you." Pa smoothed his hair back with his hand. "You've been very far away for a long time."

Jenny still didn't say anything.

"But something happened last night. Some explosion inside." He was watching her face. "That's what it looked like. That's why you're here today, right?"

"Yes," she said in a small voice. They were silent again. She took a deep breath and started talking.

"I remember when the summer started, I felt very strange and lost. It was partly John. He changed so much over the last year, and he kept leaving me out of everything. Even with the hole. He knew he needed me to dig, but he planned it with Charley. So I felt strange and disconnected from the family." She glanced at Pa. He was staring at something across the room. "And Charley was no help. He lived in his own world with his notebook and Moses. Sometimes I wanted to shake him. Then John went away and Lucy went off to her camp and Moses was killed. And there was just me and Charley. It sounds crazy, but Charley and I had never really talked to each other before. He resented me and John always doing things together and I—" She stopped. "I guess I just never thought much about him." She thought about that for a minute. "If Moses hadn't been killed, I wonder whether we would have been the same way as before. Not really paying much attention to each other."

Pa didn't answer. He knew she was asking herself the question.

"So when Charley was moping in his room, I tried to get him interested in the hole. I thought if he *did* something instead of just sitting there, he would forget about Moses a little. He wrote a story about it and read it to me one night out in the treehouse. It was very good," she said, looking at Pa. "He writes very well."

"He's never shown me anything," Pa said quietly.

"Maybe if you asked him, he would. He doesn't think you really care about what he does. He says you can't forget about the asthma."

Pa didn't say anything.

"The story took some of the hurt away, I guess. Like sucking the poison out. He came down to the hole the next morning, and we were there together every day after that. Just the two of us. And we started talking to each other. About the family and God and Moses and his fish. You know, just everything. It was crazy. Two people who had lived in the same place for thirteen years suddenly turned around and noticed each other."

Pa shifted his position on the couch. He was following the story from his side, thinking about the questions she had brought to him over the summer. So much had been going on.

140

"It was the hole. It brought us together every day. We never really thought about why we were doing it. None of us go down there now except John. It was just a reason to see each other. In the beginning, we had to make up an excuse to spend so much time together. We just couldn't admit that we enjoyed it." She smiled to herself. Talking about it like this made everything so much clearer. "And I lost that wandering feeling I had all through the beginning of the summer. Except I didn't notice it until later."

Someone ran up the steps to the porch and went inside. She held her breath. If someone came in now, she could never start again. Pa touched her arm. "It's all right," he said with a smile. "They won't come in. You're the only one who's allowed."

"The time went along like that, but we were changing without noticing it. Depending on each other. Thinking about each other in a different sort of way. It wasn't just me. It was Charley too. There was a kind of tension." She took a deep breath. "He came up one night and read me the story about Moses again. Except it was all changed. It was about me and the way I had comforted him. And I started to cry. And we reached out for each other and—"

Pa didn't say anything. He was looking out the window.

"We hugged each other for a long time." She curled her knees up against her chest. "We had been moving toward it all those weeks. This family, we never touch each other, we never reach out. Charley and I both needed that hugging. We had been waiting for it." She didn't know what Pa was thinking. His expression did not change. "It wasn't any more than that. He left me there and he went away. We never talked about it, but after that the tension seemed to get

141

bigger. I dreamed about Charley a lot." She sighed. "Then Lucy came home. Everything changed. She saw all the changes in Charley too, and she decided she wanted to catch him. She kept planning it in front of me. And I began to hate her. Charley fell for it. And there I was, left out again."

Pa looked at her. "A kind of bitter look settled on your face after Lucy came home. I remember seeing it and wondering."

"I couldn't tell her why. I couldn't tell her I was in love with my brother." There, she had said it.

"Jenny, I—"

"Wait, Pa, there's more," she said grimly. "Let me finish everything."

He nodded and sat back again. His face looked tight and angry. He doesn't want to hear any more, she decided. But he has to hear it all, because I don't have anyone else.

"We finished the hole. That was hard for me and Charley. Suddenly the whole reason for our summer was gone. Except for Charley there was something else. Someone else. I asked him if he wanted to spend one night together down in the hole. As a special celebration. Just the two of us. He liked the idea, so we took down sleeping bags and candles and some food, and he brought a bottle of wine." She paused for a minute. "I remember, all that day I kept thinking he was going to tell someone about our plan. Or that something was going to spoil it. I didn't realize until later how much I was counting on that one time alone with him. As if I thought I could change everything back. As if there were anything to go back to," she admitted softly. Her throat felt as if it were closing up. Pa took her hand and held it very tight. She could not look at his face, so she talked to the opposite wall.

"At first it was just like the other times. We talked about the hole and John and dying. We drank the whole bottle of wine, I think, and I remember feeling sort of numb. Charley asked me about sex. When I had found out about it. Then when we lay down to go to sleep, I put my head on his shoulder. It felt so warm and comfortable just to have his arm around me again. I just wanted that feeling again." She stared at Pa's face for a second and then looked away again.

"What did Charley do?"

"He pushed me away. He said people would think it was funny. After all, I was his sister. But there was a little moment when he left me there on his shoulder, as if he were considering it. It wasn't all me, Pa. He enjoyed it too."

It was all said at last. She pulled her hand away and put her head down on the arm of the sofa. The room felt smaller and closer, as if the walls were moving toward them. She didn't feel like crying anymore. It scared her to think about what Pa was going to say, but the worst part was over. She was no longer bursting with that guilty ache inside.

Pa stood up and walked over to his desk. He banged on the window at a robber squirrel and watched as it bounded away. The late sun was shining in patches on the floor. He took a deep breath and sat down beside her again.

"These last few weeks must have been awful for you," he said quietly.

She nodded. "First I hated everybody, and I kept telling myself that I didn't need anybody, that I liked being alone all the time. But after a while, I realized I was just trying to convince myself. All those nights up in the treehouse, I wanted to be down on the porch with all of you. And I was mad at myself for wanting it." She sighed. "And then I got down to the guilt. I tried to go to confession, but it didn't work. I ran out in the middle. That priest didn't know what I was talking about. I just didn't believe in what I was doing anymore. Ma would be sad if she knew that."

Pa nodded. "I don't know what to say to you, Jenny. Except that you've made all this a lot bigger than it is. You and Charley did change a lot this summer. You grew closer together, and what happened to you both sounds natural to me."

"But what if Charley hadn't stopped it?" she whispered. "I would have let it go on."

"Let's get out of here," he said quickly. "I feel stifled."

She followed him out of the house, wondering whether he was going to try and answer her question. They went down the porch steps and over the wall. The hole was empty. One of the buckets clanked mournfully against the tree in the evening breeze. Already some of the leaves were turning yellow.

"What's today, Pa?" Jenny asked suddenly as they picked their way slowly down the hill.

"September 10," he called over his shoulder.

"School starts in just a week," she said in amazement. "I've lost so much time."

They crossed the stream at the bottom of the hill and came out on the street. Jenny moved up beside Pa. It felt great to be outside again.

"I feel stiff," she said.

"You've been sitting inside for a long time," he said,

smiling down at her. "Flabby muscles," he said, squeezing her arm. "It doesn't take long."

"I bet I couldn't fill one bucket today," she grinned. "Who cares? I never want to see another bucket or another shovel. No more holes or cellars or sewers. I'm going to live aboveground for a while."

He burst out laughing. "That sounds like my old Jenny."

Her unfolding went on for days. She spent the days riding her bicycle, stretching out the cramps, exploring in wider and wider circles. In the late afternoons she and Pa would go for long walks, looking at houses and talking. She came back into the family, slowly and shyly, and they were careful with her. "As if they're scared I might suddenly go funny again," she said to Pa one afternoon.

"You won't," Pa said simply.

"It's like we're all in the playground taking turns on a seesaw," she explained carefully. "Most of the time one person is way up in the air, legs waving wildly, dizzy and out of breath. And then the other person pushes off gently and the seesaw balances for a while, each one facing the other, even, equal. But just a sigh or a word can set you off again."

He looked at her curiously. "What a picture," he said.

"I spent all summer on the seesaw with Charley," she said thoughtfully. "And then suddenly he jumped off and I came crashing down."

"And you sat there with your legs curled up under you until I came along," Pa finished.

"That's right," she said with a smile.

It was getting dark. They started up the hill toward the house. That last question was still hanging between them.

"Do you think I would have let it go on, Pa?" she asked again.

"I don't know, Jenny," he answered with a sigh. "I don't think so. You and Charley both needed each other at the same time, but that kind of needing would have passed away. Charley found someone else before you did. It could have been you first."

"I still miss him," she said softly. "I miss the talking."

"You haven't lost that. It will take a while, but you and Charley will be friends again. I'm sure he's missing you too."

"Really?" she said, looking up at him. "I never thought of that."

"One day you two will just slide back into place," Pa said, as he opened the screen door. "You might not even notice it."

Chapter Twelve

The next week Jenny went back to school. She had always looked forward to the routine of school after the freedom of the summer days. "You are a person who needs roads in your life," Mother Leclair once told her. "Otherwise you would wander too much." "That's a nice way of saying you don't apply yourself," Lucy explained sarcastically.

For a while she felt secure in the routines of the convent school, the praying and the kneeling and the curtsying to the nuns. But she knew it was just a settling time for her. She knew the summer had changed her and the change was showing.

"I argued with Mother Sessions today," she told Pa one afternoon when they were sitting out on the porch. "I was asking her about the Pope. I don't see how he can be infallible. He's just a human being like all the rest of us."

Pa looked at her sharply. "Arguing just to show you're different doesn't really prove anything."

"What do you mean?" she asked, hurt by the tone in his voice.

"Remember John," he said. "The rebel without a cause. He argued with us just because Andrew liked to fight with his parents. Don't go off making high-and-mighty statements about religion just because Charley might not believe in it anymore. Ask your own questions, Jenny. Not somebody else's."

She sat back and thought about that for a while. She saw what he meant, but she couldn't decide whether her questions were her own or Charley's. That last confession had seemed so false to her. She hadn't gone back since then.

"In the end it all comes down to faith. So often with religion, you have to accept and believe without questioning. I could never do that. Your mother does accept and believe, and sometimes I envy her for it," Pa said.

"But that's the trouble with me," Jenny cried. "I'm too accepting."

Pa smiled. "Maybe that's the way you were meant to be."

"I hope not," Jenny said fiercely.

She and Lucy avoided each other at school. They missed one another, but neither one was willing to admit it. We're both too proud, Jenny decided much later.

Lucy still spent a lot of time with Charley. They talked about Jenny sometimes. They were both missing her.

"Funny how she changed so suddenly," Lucy said. "One day she was all curled up inside herself, and the next day

148

she was talking to us again. Not like before, but she just didn't act so crazy anymore."

"It took a whole week," Charley said, thinking back over it. After the scream, he thought. "It was because of Pa," he added out loud. "She went and talked to Pa. I saw them once in his office. None of the rest of us are allowed in there without an invitation, but now Jenny's different."

"This was our changing summer," Lucy said slowly. "John changed, you and Jenny changed. Even I changed. Everybody except your mother. And mine."

"Maybe mothers never change," Charley said, thinking of that night he had tried to tell Ma about Jenny.

"What an awful thought," Lucy said.

"I didn't really mean it," he said sadly.

Sometimes Jenny would forget and run to tell Charley something, but she always stopped herself. He wouldn't be interested, she would say to herself. Often she went to John instead.

"Do you think we could build an extension on the tree-house?" she asked him one afternoon when they were down in the cellar together. "I want to make a walkway so I can go right on the roof instead of having to jump all the time."

"You've been jumping?" he asked in surprise. "That's a long way to jump."

She liked the concern in his voice. "I figured it out this summer," she said. "It's all right if you get a running start and push off with your right foot." She shrugged. "I was just proving something to myself. I don't need to do it anymore."

He pulled out a piece of paper and started drawing it up. "We'd better build something," he said gruffly. "I don't want you to fall and break your neck. Somehow it would be blamed on me."

She smiled. John still needed his excuses.

It only took them two days to build it. Pa came up to do the inspection when it was all finished.

"If Ma and I just left you three children alone, you would probably tear down this house and build it all over again," he said with a smile.

"It's called property improvement, Pa," John said.

"I hope the tax assessor doesn't come around again," Pa said, jumping up and down lightly on the new crossway. "What with the hole and the treehouse, my taxes would probably be doubled."

Things are a lot looser between John and Pa, Jenny thought happily. They know how to kid with each other again.

"Seems fine to me," Pa said. He leaned over and looked underneath. "I'm glad you put in that extra truss," he said.

"You know Jenny used to jump across here," John said. He sounded proud.

Pa looked at her sternly. "No, I didn't know that," he said quietly.

She shrugged. "I was careful, Pa." She remembered the one time she had slipped. That all seemed so long ago now.

Then one afternoon it happened. Things between Jenny and Charley just clicked back into place. When Jenny thought about it later, she wondered whether Charley had come looking for her before. Proud people do the meanest things to each other, she decided.

That afternoon Jenny came home from school and piled her books up on her desk. She was crawling out to the treehouse when she heard Charley calling for her. She stopped and listened. He sounded excited.

"Jenny, Jenny. Where are you?" He burst into the room. "Come look," he shouted. "My fish had babies. Hundreds of them. I didn't even know she was pregnant." He stopped, startled by the look of surprise on her face. They stared at each other silently, remembering how things stood between them.

"God, Charley," Jenny said slowly. "Only you could have a pregnant fish and not even know it." She smiled at him.

He laughed. "Come on, don't just stand there," he cried, dragging her out of the room. "We have to move the babies into another aquarium before the mother eats them. She's a cannibal."

She let him pull her along. Inside she was laughing.

"It does take a long time," she told Pa later. "But after a while, we just missed each other too much. He came to tell me about his pregnant fish. Nobody else. He came looking for me."

Pa burst out laughing.

"What's wrong?" she said.

"Oh, I think it's great, Jenny," he said quickly. "It just sounded funny. About the pregnant fish, I mean."

It did sound funny. She liked the way Pa's eyes crinkled up when he laughed.

"You know what, Pa?"

"What?" he said absentmindedly, as he smoothed out a drawing on his desk.

"When your eyes laugh, they look like Rice Krispies," she said solemnly.

He blushed. "You're a nut," he said. "I can't get any work done with you around. Go on. Get out of here."

She walked to the door. "I have one more thing to say," she announced.

He looked up.

"I think you and Ma should hold hands and kiss in front of us. A little demonstration of affection never hurt anyone," she added with a giggle.

"Out!" he roared, pointing at the door and laughing at the same time.

She fled upstairs, calling for Charley.

Format by Kohar Alexanian
Set in 11 pt. Times Roman